Hannah stepped closer to Adam. "You should go lie down and rest."

"I should do som

She shook he a fierce clobbering, and Besides, those men migh. If they see you outside y'll come back, and next time they might not let you ___ She didn't want to mention that the men might also not be too happy that Chesny and the others had lied to them.

Adam blew out a heavy sigh. "All right, but when I'm better, I want to do something around here to help out. I'm used to pulling my own weight—not taking charity."

Hannah lifted her chin. "It's not charity to save a man's life."

"I just don't like hiding behind a bunch of women's skirts or being in that cave." He motioned toward the secret room.

"Well, those *skirts* and that *cave* may have just saved your life for a second time."

He held her gaze for a long moment, then turned and ambled back down the stairs. She watched for a moment and shut the door. She supposed she wouldn't like being stuck in the hole alone either, but he could at least show a little gratitude.

She spun away, determined to check on her dog and put the mysterious stranger from her mind, but with each step she took, his scent traveled with her. The feel of his arms around her warmed her from the inside out. Would hugging Jamie feel as. . .wonderful?

As much as she wished it were so, she didn't think it would.

VICKIE McDONOUGH believes God is the ultimate designer of romance. She is a wife of thirty-six years, mother to four grown sons, and a doting grandma. When not writing, she enjoys reading, watching movies, and traveling. Visit Vickie's website at www.vickiemcdonough.com.

Books by Vickie McDonough

HEARTSONG PRESENTS

Secrets
of the Heart

Vickie McDonough

Heartsong Presents

A note from the Author:
I love to hear from my readers! You may correspond with me by writing:

Vickie McDonough
Author Relations
PO Box 721
Uhrichsville, OH 44683

ISBN 978-1-61626-372-0

SECRETS OF THE HEART

All scripture quotations are taken from the King James Version of the Bible.

All of the characters and events in this book are fictitious. Any resemblance to actual persons, living or dead, or to actual events is purely coincidental.

Our mission is to publish and distribute inspirational products offering exceptional value and biblical encouragement to the masses.

PRINTED IN THE U.S.A.

one

The hairs on the back of Cooper Reed's neck stood on end. He peered over his shoulder and reined his tired horse to a stop, straining to hear the sound he'd heard a moment ago. Nothing moved in the woods behind him. Nothing but the trees dancing in the light spring breeze. The wind swished through pine branches above, and a waxwing whistled from a nearby bush. Overhead, a hawk screeched. Cooper glanced up at the bird soaring high in the sky, without a care in the world. He heaved a sigh and pulled his gaze back to the trail. Had he finally lost the men pursuing him?

Coop's horse jerked its head up, ears flicked forward, and stared back the way they'd just come. The animal snorted and pranced sideways. A shiver charged down Coop's spine. A tree limb snapped, intruding on the peaceful scene, and hoofbeats pounded toward him.

He reined his horse around and slapped the leather against his mount's shoulder. "He-yah!" The animal leaped forward, in spite of its exhaustion, and stretched to a gallop. Coop's hand went instinctively to the pouch tucked into his waistband—the pouch that held his precious cargo. He had to see it safely to his father.

"Halt, or suffer the consequences!" a shout heralded behind him.

He hunkered over his mount's neck, knowing that stopping most likely meant death. A shot rang out. He ducked, and the

5

lead ball whizzed past his ear. Soon he'd be on Reed land. He had to reach home. He had to reveal the traitor among his father's friends.

Up ahead, Coop could see the open fields of Reed Springs. Not a soul was in sight. Perhaps he should have headed to the Madisons. They were his parents' best friends and closest neighbors. Though he hadn't seen them in years, he could get help there, but seeking their assistance could endanger them, and he couldn't risk that. He urged his horse to run faster.

Shooting a man on horseback was difficult, but once he reached the fields, he'd be a clear target, without the cover of the trees. His heartbeat kept time with his mount's thundering hooves. He needed to get rid of his cargo. If those men caught him, they would find it, and he'd have no proof to back up his accusations.

His mind raced for a solution, and suddenly he knew the answer. He lifted his gaze, searching the edge of the approaching tree line and found the exact spot where he, Jamie, and Michael Madison had hidden when they were hunting deer. The logs they'd piled up had grayed and partially collapsed, but the shadowy interior would be the perfect hiding place. He yanked the leather pouch from his waistband and flung it sideways, praying his pursuers didn't notice. All the times he'd played there as a boy, he never once considered it might one day harbor a dreadful secret.

His horse plunged out of the trees. Down the hill and up ahead, the cotton field spread far and wide. Coop's mount flicked his ears forward, slowing his pace as they raced down the steep hill, toward the quickly approaching creek that separated the field from the woodlands.

"C'mon, boy." Cooper hoped the horse could keep going. Just another half mile or so, and he'd be home. Safe.

Another shot blasted behind him. The horse squealed, staggered, and fell to his knees. Coop flew over the animal's neck, and his head and shoulder collided with the hard ground. He rolled over and over, pain surging through his body. Finally he stilled at the edge of the creek, and water seeped into his pants. He blinked open his eyes. His horse, blood seeping from his left thigh, plummeted toward him. Coop lifted his arm as the horse rolled over him.

❧

"Are you actually going to marry a man you hardly know?"

Hannah glanced at her friend sitting next to her in the buggy. "How many times are you going to ask me that, Ruthie?"

"Until you get some sense. This isn't the dark ages, you know." Ruthie Sutherland shook her head, tucked up a strand of light brown hair that had come loose, then redid the tie of her straw hat.

"No, but parents do still arrange marriages. Sometimes." Hannah shoved down a niggle of doubt. "Besides, Jamie has always been kind and treated me respectfully. He's a handsome man with his black hair and blue eyes."

"Whatever became of that brother of his? Wasn't he lost at sea or something? What was his name?"

"Cooper. That's such a sad situation." Even though she hadn't seen Cooper Reed in many years, Hannah's heart ached at the pain his disappearance had cost the Reed family. "Jamie was devastated that they couldn't locate his brother on their trip to England."

"Un-huh, he sure 'nough was." Chesny, Hannah's former nanny and now lady's maid, nodded. "Those brothers was closer than a flea on a hound dog."

"Didn't he quit school and run off or something?"

Hannah shook her head. "I don't think that's true. Something more nefarious must have happened, I'm sure of it. Coop was a good boy, just like Jamie. Oh, he was a bit more independent and feisty, but he deeply loved his family.

He'd never go off and not leave word."

"Somethin' bad done happened to that boy."

"I certainly hope not," Hannah said. "The Reeds sent word that they had found no clue as to what happened to him. They extended their time in England but are now returning because of the wedding."

"At least the Reeds are wealthy. And if that other son doesn't return, you'll be all the richer." Ruthie fanned her face with her hand, not looking the least bit sorry for her coldhearted words.

"Ruthie! What a horrible thing to say." Hannah could hardly believe some of the things that fell from her friend's lips. "I pray every night that Cooper will be found and returned to his family unharmed."

"You probably wouldn't even recognize the man if he passed you on the street. How long has he been away?"

"More than seven years. He served aboard one of his father's ships before finally deciding to attend college in England. He was your age—sixteen—I believe, when he left." Hannah pressed a fold of her apron with her fingers. What could have befallen Cooper Reed? The family had not received a request for ransom, so a kidnapping had been ruled out. Had Coop lost his temper and gotten in a fight and killed? It was all such a mystery and cast a pale on her wedding plans, but she would cancel them in a moment's notice if it meant Coop's safe return. *Please, Lord. Return him to his family. Keep Cooper safe until that day. And please comfort the Reeds and give them hope.*

"Well, at least the Reeds have this big plantation and that shipping business and exquisite house in Charleston. Oh!" Ruthie gasped and turned in the seat. "If you live in town, we can see each other every day."

Hannah glanced across the seat and caught her former nanny's gaze. Chesny rolled her dark eyes and adjusted her colorful head wrap. Hannah bit back a grin and tried to act more enthusiastic than she felt. Ruthie was a dear friend, but she was several years younger and of an outgoing nature that grated on Hannah's nerves after spending two weeks together. She searched her mind for a truthful response. "That would be nice, but I plan to live on the plantation most of the time."

"Oh pooh." Ruthie fell back against the seat, her arms crossed. "Why ever would you want to live out here? There's nothing but dirt and—and—cotton."

Staring out at the fields, Hannah tried to see the plantation from her friend's eyes. The cotton seedlings were only a half-foot tall, their green shoots waving a greeting on the warm breeze. On the other side of the buggy, abundant trees and tall grasses hugged the Ashley River that started at the Charleston Harbor and flowed miles inland. The fresh air filled her nostrils, so vastly different from the stench of Charleston on a hot day.

Ruthie nudged her with her elbow. "Well, don't you have anything to say?"

"I love it out here. It's so peaceful, and you don't have neighbors peering out their windows at you when you're sitting on your piazza."

"You're daft. That's all there is to it. Why your parents didn't make you go to school in town, I'll never know. I suppose I'll have to satisfy myself by continuing to make these treks to Madison Gardens—or rather Reed Springs—even after you are married."

Hannah shrugged. "Last I heard, Lucas Reed was going to continue searching for Cooper. Jamie will be overseeing Reed Shipping, so I'm sure we'll get to town quite often."

Ruthie smiled, contented at last. Hannah turned her attention to the tall home belonging to the Reed family as it came into view. The three-story, redbrick house rose up majestically against the bright blue sky. The wide white porch and well-manicured garden welcomed visitors. Though the structure wasn't as ornate as the Reed's Charleston house, it was much roomier.

Hannah had looked forward to being mistress of the house for as long as she could remember, and her mother had prepared her since she was young. Heather Reed and Caroline Madison had cooked up the marriage between her and Jamie shortly after her birth. Jamie always enjoyed playing with her when they were young, and as she grew, she took pleasure in seeing him whenever the family visited. Their marrying had started out as a joke among their parents, but somewhere along her childhood, the idea had taken root and grown and had become something to be expected one day.

But now that the day of her wedding was less than a month away, doubts assailed her continually. Was she making a big mistake in marrying Jamie Reed?

two

Simeon, their driver, helped the women from the buggy, then led the horses toward the back of the barn where he always parked the buggy whenever they visited Reed Springs. Hannah patted her pocket, checking to be sure the treat she'd brought for Honey was still there.

"So, what are we doing today?" Ruthie asked.

"I thought we'd air out the upstairs bedrooms, then make sure that all the linens are clean and everything's ready for the Reeds' return." Hannah waved at the west end of the house. "Let's start there. It will be cooler now than it will be this afternoon."

Chesny carried the basket that held their lunch. "I'll go on inside, Miss Hannah, and see if Maisy and Leta are he'pin' us today."

Hannah nodded. "I'll be right there as soon as I give Honey the treat I brought her."

Chesny chuckled and shook her head. "You and that ol' hoss."

"Why do you always have to visit that horse?" Ruthie crossed her arms. "And why do you let your slave tell you what she's going to do? You know you have to use a strict hand on them or they'll—"

Hannah held up her palm. "Our Negroes are not slaves; they're employees. You know that."

"I may know it but I don't have to like it. Why, it's just plain absurd—paying those people a wage. What do they need money for?"

"You sound like your father."

11

Ruthie hiked her chin. "So?"

Hannah shook her head. "Nothing. Do you want to go with me to the barn and see Honey?"

"Eww. No. I'd rather do menial labor inside than visit a smelly barn." Ruthie swirled around and stomped away.

Hannah sighed. She couldn't help thinking about what Chesny sometimes murmured when visitors were particularly peevish. *Fish and guests, they both stink after three days.*

Hannah smiled and walked toward the barn. Having guests visit the plantation and stay for an extended time was common, but she was always a bit relieved when they finally left and things could get back to normal. She pulled open the barn door, noting that the latch had not been fastened. "Israel, are you in there?"

When the Reed Springs caretaker didn't respond, she stepped inside and looked around. Dust motes floated on fingers of sunlight that poked through the cracks in the old building. Ruthie said the barn stank, but Hannah found the scent of hay and horses comforting. She'd always loved venturing out to the barn, both here and at home.

Most times when she arrived at Reed Springs, the caretaker was present. She even brought him a treat on occasion. "Israel?"

Honey lifted her head over the stall gate and nickered. Hannah lifted the skirt of her high-waisted day dress and crossed the hard-packed dirt floor to her destination. "Good morning, girl. How are you today?"

Honey bobbed her head as if to say she was fine. Hannah loved the brown mare, which she'd ridden with the Reed boys and her brother when she was small. "How's your leg today? Huh? Still bothering you?"

The horse stretched her neck and blew against Hannah's skirt. She giggled. "Ah, you found your treat, huh?"

She inserted her hand into the slit in the side of her gown, fished two big carrot chunks out of the pocket she had tied around her waist, then held them out to the horse. Honey's big lips lapped up the treat, tickling Hannah's hand. She giggled, then noticed the horse slobber on her hand. "Ruthie would scold me for certain if she saw this."

Hannah hunted around for a piece of burlap or cloth on which to clean off her hand. She pursed her lips at not finding what she needed. Hay would have to do. She crossed over to the pile of fresh hay that Israel must have forked from the overhead loft, and her shoe smacked into something hard. She looked down. Her gaze landed on a boot—with a leg attached.

The skin on Hannah's face tightened, and her heartbeat galloped like a horse running a race. The boot moved, and Hannah leaped backward, tripping on her skirt. She fell flat on her backside on the hard ground, never taking her eyes off the boot.

Suddenly, the whole pile of hay moved and a second boot slid out from under the pile. Who was under there—and how could they breathe?

The mound of hay moved again, and a ghastly moan ascended from it. Hannah forgot her bruised backside. Rolling over onto her hands and knees, she scrambled across the filthy barn floor, her gaze searching for anything she could use as a weapon. She spied an old ax handle leaning against the wall and grabbed it, then used it to help her stand. She spun back around, holding the weapon above one shoulder.

She struggled to swallow the burning sensation in her throat. The rapid pounding of her heart kept time with her staccato breathing. In the shadows, two black boots now protruded from under the edge of the hay, along with a man's muddy trousers. That man had been there the whole time she was feeding Honey.

One of the boots shifted again, and a second moan caused

the hairs on the back of her neck to stand up. She glanced at the door, knowing the smart thing would be to run back to the other women, but could she be putting them in danger? Mustering her courage, Hannah crept toward the lumpy pile of hay, keeping the handle ready in case it was needed.

Oh Lord, please help me. I don't know if I could whack a living person, even to protect myself.

Before she lost her nerve, she nudged one of the boots with the toe of her shoe. The stranger rewarded her with another groan and a raspy cough. Hannah took a shuddering breath and backed away. Maybe she should go find Israel.

But curiosity overpowered her fear. With white-knuckled hands, she clutched the ax handle and used the end to flip hay off the person. The long, lean form of a dark-haired man appeared.

She poked him in the shoulder with the handle. "Mister, are you awake?"

When he didn't respond, she knelt down to get a closer look. A thick trail of dried blood ran from his nose to his bloodied and bruised lips. Hannah took a deep breath and mentally steadied her trembling hands. She reached forward, lifted a wad of hay off the top half of the stranger's face, and tossed the debris aside. To her surprise, she discovered a young man who looked to be only slightly older than herself.

"That's a nasty gash you've got over your eye," she whispered. "You won't be seeing out of it until that swelling goes down." Hannah shook her head. The man needed help, not an inventory of his wounds. She stood and turned her back to the man, lifted her skirt, and quickly untied the double pocket from around her waist. The linen fabric would serve well as a bandage until she could get the stranger to the house.

"I'm going to wrap your head wound now." She doubted he could hear her, but maybe the tone of her voice would somehow comfort him. She brushed aside most of his dark brown hair, which was littered with pieces of grass. Then she folded the fabric, placed one pocket over the lump on his forehead, wrapped the tie around his head, and secured it.

She sat back, ready to go get Chesny, but then decided she'd better check for broken bones before they moved the man. Wasn't that what her father said to do when Michael had fallen from a tree and injured himself? Thankfully, her brother had only bruises and scrapes. She reached toward the stranger's leg, pausing in a moment of uncertainty, then gently ran her hands down the length of it, checking for swelling. A breath of relief slipped from her lips at finding none.

She ran her hand along his firm shoulder then cut a path down his forearm to his wrist. Her hand lingered a moment on his warm, calloused palm. She lifted his arm, turning it over to examine his dirty, scraped knuckles. It was a strong, tanned hand, accustomed to hard work.

"What in the world happened to you? If you were in a fight, I certainly hope you were on the right side of the law." She laid his hand down to his side and leaned over the stranger's chest to check his other arm. As she reached out, he erupted in a coughing spasm and drew up his right leg. Hannah jerked her arm back, but the man's knee rammed into her shoulder, throwing her off balance. Unable to stop her momentum, the full weight of her body landed hard across his solid chest.

"Aahhh, you t–trying to k–kill me?" the man cried in a hoarse voice. Fast as lightning, his left hand snaked out, grabbing her upper arm. He pushed her body off his.

Hannah screamed. She struggled to free her arm, but the man's rock-hard grasp didn't yield. The strength in his bruised body amazed her. She cast a glance at the ax handle, which lay just out of reach.

Swallowing with difficulty, she found her voice and stopped struggling. "You'd b—better let me go, if you know what's good for you." She hoped she sounded braver than she felt. Could the stranger hear her pounding heart, racing like a ship in a stiff wind?

The man stared at her, his dark eyebrows furrowed into a single brow. With short, choppy breaths, he fought for air. Hannah squirmed against his hold as he watched her with his open eye.

Why hadn't she thought about him possibly having broken ribs? Knowing she caused him such discomfort when she fell on him concerned her nearly as much as the fact that he still held her captive.

After a moment, his tense expression eased, and he relaxed. She caught herself licking her lips as she watched him try to wet his dry, cracked lips with his tongue.

"W—water," he croaked as he released her.

Hannah rubbed her aching arm. She doubted the man meant to hurt her, but she would carry the bruises he'd surely inflicted for a long while. As her fear ebbed, she eyed the man with growing compassion. He must be in terrible pain. She stood, looking for the bucket of water Israel generally kept handy.

"Don't go. I w—won't hurt you. Need water, p—please." He reached toward the bandage on his forehead with his filthy hand.

Hannah grabbed his arm and pulled it back down. "Don't touch that. I put a bandage on your head wound. Just hold on a bit, and I'll be back shortly with some water."

She located the bucket in the corner and carried the dipper back to the stranger. He attempted to push up on one elbow but then sucked in a sudden gasp as pain etched his face. He pressed his hand to his side.

"Here, let me help you." Taking care not to spill the water,

Hannah stooped down and slipped her hand behind his head, lifting it just enough that he could slurp up the water.

He grunted and laid his head down. His lips tightened into a thin white line, and he scrunched his eyes shut. "Who are y–you?"

"My name is Hannah Madison, and my family lives on the neighboring plantation, just over a mile away. Who are you, and what are you doing here, might I ask?"

The man stared up at her with a dazed look. He pressed his fingertips against the uninjured side of his brow. "I—I don't know."

"What do you mean?"

He squeezed his forehead. Pain and confusion engulfed his battered face. "Don't know how I got here. Can't remember."

three

Hannah stepped back and narrowed her eyes. Could he be telling the truth? Perhaps he was a thief hiding from pursuers. Or a servant who'd suffered a beating at the hand of the man he worked for and then run away. But his confusion didn't look faked.

A Bible story her mother had once read during evening devotions blazed across her mind like a wildfire. The Good Samaritan helped the wounded man on the side of the road. Hannah had few opportunities to help others outside of those living on her family's plantation. This was her chance to put those biblical truths into action.

"Do you know where you are?"

The man looked around again. For the first time, a hint of a smile tugged at his puffy lips. "Looks rather a lot like a barn, best I can tell with one eye." Then the smile disappeared, and a scowl replaced it. Glancing down, he grabbed a wad of hay off his shirt and tossed it aside. "Daft, is it not? A grown man who doesn't even know where he is."

"I'm sure it will all come back to you. It looks as if you took a hard blow to the head, and I've heard that can cause a person to be disoriented."

He stared at her a brief moment, then turned his face away. The man's helplessness and confusion obviously embarrassed him. His calloused hands and muscular frame proved he was a man accustomed to taking care of himself. What could have happened to him?

"Shhh. Don't fret," she whispered, hoping to reassure him. "I need to get some help, then get you inside the house and clean up your injuries. There's dirt and pieces of hay in your wounds. You might even need some suturing to close up that nasty gash on your head."

He looked at her again. "I don't fret."

Hannah's lips twitched. Men and their need to appear strong. Her father and brother acted the same. "Ah, my mistake. But at least you remembered that." She stood and stepped back. "A big, strong man like you doesn't need any help, right?"

"That's not what I said."

She spun around. He may not want her help, but he needed it. And she needed to find Israel.

"Wait! You're not leaving me here, are you?" he whispered.

Remorse twisted in her stomach at causing him distress. She shouldn't have poked fun at him. She faced him again. "Tell me, what's your name?"

The man pressed on the bandage covering his right brow and gazed up at her with his uninjured eye. Hannah's heart lurched at the panic and vulnerability in his expression. His hoarse whisper broke the silence. "I—I can't remember."

"You can't remember your own name?" She reached out to comfort him.

He shook his head. Utter despair encompassed his battered face.

❧

"I declare, you have all the luck. Imagine finding such a finely built man in a barn." Ruthie stamped her foot and crossed her arms. "Why couldn't this have happened when I first arrived instead of the day before I return home?"

Hannah and Ruthie stood outside the closed bedroom door while Israel and Chesny washed the stranger and helped him into an old nightshirt that had belonged to Mr. Reed. They had wrapped his chest before moving him, but even with help, the long walk from the barn had exhausted the man.

"Who do you suppose he is?"

Hannah shrugged. "I don't know. He can't remember his name or how he got to the barn."

Ruthie's hazel eyes widened, and she clapped her hands. "I do love a good mystery." She tapped her index finger on her lips. "Perhaps he's the son of a king, traveling to meet his princess and was attacked and the treasure stolen." She gasped. "Oh, what if the ruffians kidnapped the princess?"

Hannah smiled and shook her head. "That's some imagination you have."

"Ooo, no, what if he is the kidnapper and has hidden away the princess for a ransom? Why, she could be locked away somewhere all alone."

Hannah sighed. "Or perhaps he's just a man traveling on business."

"Then how did he get all beat up?"

The door opened, and they both stepped back. Hannah's gaze shot past Chesny to the stranger. "How is he?"

She shook her head. "Not so good. Someone done beat him up real bad."

"You just have them wimmenfolk fetch me if'n you needs anythin'." Israel told the stranger; then he backed away from the bed.

When Israel stepped out of the room, Hannah motioned him to follow, and she walked the short hall to the upstairs sitting room. She glanced at Chesny and Israel. "Have either of you seen that man before?"

Israel shook his head. "No, Miz Hannah. I never did."

Chesny didn't respond for a moment. "I thought maybe there was somethin' familiar about that boy, but I dunno. He just too busted up to tell."

Hannah glanced back toward the stranger's door where Ruthie stood, peering in. Perhaps in the better light of the house she might recognize the man, although he hadn't seemed at all familiar before.

Maisy plodded up the stairs, carrying a cream-colored pitcher with blue flowers on it. "Where y'all want this here water?"

Hannah pointed the way. "Maisy, did you find any bandages?"

"No, Miz Hannah, but Leta, she be lookin' in some other places."

Hannah nodded. "All right. Bring them up as soon as you locate them—and some medicinal salve, if you have any."

"Yes'm." Maisy disappeared into the bedroom.

"Chesny, would you please set some water to boil and see if there's any fresh meat we can stew to make some broth?"

"I can go an' catch a chick'n," Israel offered.

Hannah nodded. "That would be nice. Thank you." She spun around to head into the bedroom when a hand on her arm stopped her.

"Just where you be goin', Miz Hannah?" Chesny stared at her with brows lifted.

"Why, to doctor my patient, of course."

"I'll help her," Ruthie added.

"Un-uh, t'ain't proper." Shaking her head, Chesny shoved her hands to her hips.

Hannah lifted her chin. "And why not? Mama often doctors our family and workers who get hurt. It's one of the duties of the plantation's mistress."

"You ain't the mistress of *this* house yet, and besides, yo' mama, she be a married woman."

Hannah blushed, wondering just what Chesny thought she would do. "There's nothing improper about it. The man is completely covered with a nightshirt and a sheet. You and Israel have taken care of his ribs. I just plan to tend the wounds on his face."

"And I'm going to help her," Ruthie stated again, as if no one had heard her before. She crossed the hall and stood beside Hannah and joined her in staring at Chesny.

The older woman shook her head and trod toward the stairs. "It just ain't right, if'n you asks me, but them girls, they ain't askin'. They's just tellin'."

Israel nodded and followed Hannah's maid down the stairs.

Ruthie leaned toward her and grinned. "You told her. I didn't think you had it in you." She sashayed toward the bedroom door with the long skirt of her high-waisted gown flowing behind her.

Chesny stopped on the stairs, and Israel almost smacked into her. She glanced back at Hannah. "I'm'a goin' to the kitchen like you done asked, but then I'm'a comin' back to that man's room. It just ain't proper fo' two wimmen to be alone with him."

Hannah wasn't sure what had gotten into her, but she didn't like upsetting Chesny. She rarely butted heads with the older woman, who had been her nanny since she was a young girl but now was more of a friend and confidante. It was an odd relationship for the daughter of a plantation owner and a black servant, but she didn't want it to be any other way. She'd grown up despising slavery. Her family and the Reeds were among the few plantation owners who paid their Negro workers a wage. They were employees, not slaves. She just had to overlook Chesny's bossiness at times. The woman was only watching out for her.

❧

A pretty lady strolled into the room—no, not a lady, but rather an adolescent not more than fifteen or sixteen, he'd guess. He looked past her, hoping the other woman would return—the one who'd found him in the barn.

The girl looked at him and grimaced. She twisted her lips, then spun away and busied herself with opening a window. He sighed and turned his face toward the wall. What must he look like to repulse her so?

From the waist up, every part of him ached. He could only

take slow and shallow breaths or risk stabbing pains in his side. His head pounded, and his face felt like mush. What had happened to him?

Why couldn't he remember anything further back than awakening in that barn? Who was he? Where had he come from?

He clenched a wad of the fresh-smelling sheet in his hand. Efforts to remember only brought sharp pains to his head. Perhaps the woman—Hannah Madison—was correct. Time would heal him. He had to believe that. He couldn't live in this fog forever.

A gentle touch on the top of his hand drew his gaze. Ah, Miss Madison—or perhaps it was *Mrs.* Madison—had returned.

"Are you in pain?"

He shook his head, then grimaced. Vision blurred, and his head felt as if a horse had sat on it.

She patted his hand. "Try to relax and rest. I'm going to clean up your wounds; then we'll leave you alone so you can sleep. Later, we'll have some broth for you."

"Broth—that's a weak soup, is it not?"

She nodded.

"Why is it I can remember something as trivial as broth but not more important issues like who I am?" He hated the confusion fogging his mind and this feeling of helplessness. He couldn't even sit up without assistance.

"It is an odd thing, but I trust that God will restore your health and your memories."

God. He hadn't thought about God since coming to. He laid his head back and stared out the window at the soft blue sky, not all that certain what he believed about the Creator. Perhaps God would be merciful and do as the kind woman said and restore him.

Unless, of course, God was punishing him for some horrible deed he had done.

four

Hannah moistened the cloth, then gently wiped the dried blood from the stranger's face. She removed the bandage from the wound above his eye, examined the injury, then laid her hand on the man's forearm. "This might hurt a bit."

He breathed out a slow sigh, then nodded.

Hannah worked carefully, dampening the wounded area. After a few moments, the blood softened, and she pulled a lock of dark hair out of the gash on the stranger's eyebrow.

"*Owww!* Take it easy!" The man grabbed her wrist again. Hannah stared down at him with her brows lifted, and he quickly released her.

"I'm sorry that hurt. Just hold still a bit longer and I'll be finished." She remoistened the cloth. With one hand, she held the man's stubbly chin, and with the other, she carefully wiped the remaining blood off his nose and lips.

She glanced up and discovered his intense gaze on her face, mere inches away from his. His good eye—a grayish blue—studied her, and his warm breath tickled her cheek. The intensity in his stare made her hand shake. She straightened, keeping her features composed. Tearing her gaze away from his, she focused on cleaning his lips. They'd be nice lips when they healed.

Hannah sucked in a gasp. Where in the world had that thought come from? It was hardly a decent thought for a woman preparing to be married.

Ruthie stepped away from the window across the room. "How can you stand to do such a menial, disgusting task? Why not let your Negro do it?"

How could Ruthie be so insensitive? "I'm merely offering Christian charity by tending this man's wounds. Would you have me ignore his pain because the task is unpleasant?"

"I would have you back at your house sipping tea in the parlor if it was up to me. I'm going downstairs. It stinks in here."

Stunned, Hannah watched her friend flounce from the room. Ruthie was immature, but she'd never known her to be so cruel and uncaring, except where slaves were concerned—and that strong opinion had been expertly cultivated by her outspoken father. Hannah had worked hard to get her friend to see Negroes as real people with emotions, but Ruthie only thought of them as property. Such a sad thing for people to be so heartless where others were concerned.

Something brushed the back of Hannah's hand, and she glanced down. The man's fingers were just inches from hers.

"Could I have some more water, please?"

"Certainly." Hannah poured fresh water from the pitcher into a glass Maisy had brought up earlier. He lifted his head and rested his palm against the back of her hand, warming it. Hannah's heart thumped hard as she stared at his hand on hers. Finally, he lay back.

"I need to know what happened to me."

"Can you remember anything about that? Did you take a fall off your horse, or perhaps you met up with some scoundrels who robbed and beat you?"

"No. . .uh, I don't know—" He coughed and grabbed his chest.

"Shh, there now," she said, patting his shoulder. "We can talk about this later. Right now, you need to rest."

Hannah pulled her arm away and poured a generous amount of water on a clean cloth. Folding it, she placed it over the man's eye. "Hold that right there. The coolness of the water will help the swelling to go down."

She started to walk away, but the stranger reached out and grabbed her wrist. He groaned from the effort. "I'm not always this helpless."

"I'm sure you aren't." She glanced at his wide shoulders and strong hands, then pulled her gaze away from her shameless study. Her cheeks warmed. "Get some sleep now, and we'll figure out everything else later. I'm so sorry this happened to you. I remember when one of our workers found two white men stealing from our barn. The thieves attacked Jasper when he tried to stop them. One man hit him in the head with a shovel and left him for dead. His head had been badly injured, and I thought for sure he would die. For weeks, he didn't know a single one of us, not even his wife and children."

"That would be rough. I don't think I have children." He gazed up at the ceiling as if thinking deeply. "Surely I'd remember if I did."

"I would hope so. You'll be encouraged to know our worker's memory came back after a few weeks. Yours will, too, I would imagine. Just give it some time. In the meantime, you can stay here, and we'll take good care of you until you're up and about again."

"Thank you. I do appreciate your kindness."

Hannah smiled and nodded, then backed away. Already he'd closed his eyes and looked more relaxed. She turned and came to a halt when she saw Chesny standing just inside the door.

"I done brung up them bandages and the salve. Maisy and Leta are fixin' to pluck that chick'n Israel done killed. They'll make chick'n soup that we'all kin eat."

"That sounds nice. I'll go check on Ruthie. She seems more out of sorts than normal."

Chesny snorted. "That girl, she always got a beehive under her skirts."

"I suspect, she's probably just upset at returning home tomorrow. She won't admit it, but she likes being at Madison Gardens."

"Humph. I sure cain't tell by how she acts." Chesny leaned toward Hannah and nudged her chin toward the bed. "That stranger, he be a learned man."

Hannah turned back to her patient. Now that she thought about it, he didn't have the dialect of a common-born man. She wasn't certain, but she thought she'd detected a faint English accent.

Her eyes widened. What if he was an Englishman come to stir up trouble? Talk about there being another war with England ran rampant these days. What if he was a spy?

❧

"What do you mean you lost him?"

Sam smoothed his bushy moustache and cast a wary glance toward the man he knew only as Boss. Average in height, with a belly resembling a pregnant woman's late in her term, Boss preferred telling others what to do rather than doing things himself. Boss only answered to one man, and Sam had no idea who that was, but as long as he was paid for his work, he didn't care.

"Jeeter was a bit rough on the kid," Sam said. "When he wouldn't talk, Jeeter punched him in the face and kicked him in the side a couple times."

"He didn't feel nuthin'. He was already mostly dead from that fall off his horse." Jeeter said, spewing a stream of tobacco spit on the ground, mere inches from Boss's dusty boots.

Boss jumped back four inches, almost too much for his rotund frame. "Jeeter, you idiot."

Sam stifled the laugh rising up within. Boss reminded him of a chicken with clipped wings as his beefy arms flapped and he wrestled to regain his footing.

"You spit on my new boots, and I'll knock the tar out of you. I didn't want that kid killed, at least not until I found who he told what to. Mr. S. won't be happy about this." Boss removed his hat and smoothed out his thinning strands of hair in a futile attempt to cover his balding head. Cramming his hat back on, he turned to Sam. "Did you search him?"

"Yeah, Boss." Sam studied the dust on his own boots to avoid Boss's scrutinizing gaze. "We went clean through his clothes and the saddlebags of that horse he stole. There wasn't nuthin' there," he muttered, twisting the end of his bushy moustache.

"You sure you got the right kid?" Boss asked.

"Well, I reckon," Jeeter scratched his chest. "We found him at a tavern in Charleston not long after he jumped ship. Would'a caught him then if he hadn't seen us come in the door. He climbed on the nearest table and jumped out a window. Was down the road and nearly out of sight on that stolen horse before we could get out the door."

"Don't you keep those shanghaied sailors locked up when you make port?" Boss yanked off his hat again and slapped it against his leg. A small cloud of dust floated down to the ground. "I still don't see how he got away once you caught him."

"It took most of the day to catch up with him, and we only did then because his horse gave out. The kid was out cold all evening, so we bedded down for the night. Jeeter was on watch, but he must'a nodded off." Sam glanced at the scrawny little sailor. He was nothing but an old fool as far as Sam was concerned. There was no reason for him to be so rough on the boy, but he'd taken an immediate disliking to Cooper Reed the day he was brought aboard ship.

"I did not fall asleep." Jeeter puffed up his chest, his black eyes flaming.

"Wasn't the kid tied up?" Boss asked.

"He was knocked senseless. Kicked in the head by his

horse, from the looks of it. There weren't no reason to tie him up." Jeeter curled his lip, crossed his arms over his chest.

"I told you to tie him up anyway, whil'st I got the firewood." Sam wasn't about to take the blame for something Jeeter had failed to do.

"You two lame-brain good-fer-nuthin's. You sound like a couple of kids arguin'. I should'a gone myself. Now, what am I gonna tell Mr. S.? If that kid tells anyone what he knows, we're all gonna be dead, Mr. S. will see to that. His business—and his good name—are on the line."

"The kid couldn't have got far. We scared his horse off so he was on foot, and bad as he was hurtin', he's gotta to be around here close by."

"Pack up then," Boss ordered. "We gotta find him."

❧

"Miz Hannah, somebody be comin'." Simeon slowed the buggy and glanced back over his shoulder.

Hannah lifted the large brim of her straw hat and gazed across the meadow. Squinting from the glare of the brilliant morning sun, she lifted her hand to block the light. A tall, thin man rode toward them. His thick, droopy moustache touched the bottom of his chin. His musket was drawn and rested across his lap. Hannah glanced at Chesny, seated across from her, gave her maid a brief nod, then focused her gaze on the stranger.

When the buggy stopped, two more men rode out of the trees in their direction. Hannah wished now that she'd taken her brother up on his offer to escort her to Reed Springs this morning, but with her father in Charleston, along with her mother, Michael was needed at home to oversee things. "Drive on, Simeon."

The smaller man kicked his horse, trotted over, and stopped in front of the buggy.

"Now just hold on there, ma'am. We don't mean you no

harm. Just need some information."

Hannah eyed the heavyset man who'd spoken, wondering how he'd ever managed to get on his horse. The poor animal would be swayback before the year's end, for sure. She plastered a charitable smile on her face and struggled to keep her voice steady. "What kind of information do you gentlemen need?"

"Who are you? Start with that," the fat man ordered.

Hannah stood, hoping the benefit of height would make her seem less vulnerable, and it put her closer to the muff pistol hiding under Chesny's apron, should she need it. "My name's Hannah Madison, and this is my father's land." She narrowed her eyes and glared at the third man positioned in front of the matched black geldings that pulled her buggy.

"My, my, Boss, we got us Richard Madison's girl." The small man's leering gaze roved down Hannah's body and back up.

She crossed her arms over her chest and swallowed. *Keep us safe, Lord.*

"Shut up, you fool." The man called Boss stared at her. "Look, Miss Madison. We just want to know if you've seen a stranger 'bout your age, riding a dun gelding around these parts. We've got some business to take care of with him. That's all."

"Uh. . .no. You three gentlemen are the only folks I've seen since we left home." It was true, she reasoned. She hadn't seen her stranger today—and he definitely wouldn't be riding with all his injuries. Not yet anyway. "We don't usually see too many folks way out here. 'Course we do see a trapper and an old Indian ever so often. Oh, and once in a great while, a traveling man comes past our home and sells his wares to my mother. Life on these big plantations can be lonely." Of course, not too lonely when Ruthie had just boarded a ship back to Charleston less than an hour earlier.

Hannah smiled and casually smoothed out her dress, hoping to come across like an overly friendly neighbor. While her outer demeanor remained calm, her insides were treacherously close to giving her away. Could it be possible that these three men had attacked her stranger? What could these ruffians want with him? He had nothing—no possessions of any kind that Hannah had noticed. Not even a horse or a change of clothing.

The big man snorted and rolled his eyes at the other two men. "Missy, all we want to know is if you've seen a dark-haired kid riding a big dun."

"I've already answered that, haven't I? Excuse me, gentlemen, but I'm expected somewhere soon. I can assure you that I haven't seen the man you're searching for, riding a horse or not. In fact, you're the only people I've seen riding today."

Hannah forced herself to look from man to man. Both the moustached man and the smaller one looked ready to agree, but Boss scowled at her. She kept a smile on her lips and steadily held his gaze, though she wanted nothing more than to race away like the wind.

Finally, he grunted, "I guess you don't know nothin'. We'd best be gettin' along."

"Good day, gentlemen." Hannah flashed them what she hoped was a charming smile. She sat down and eyed Chesny. The woman lifted a corner of her apron, revealing the walnut stock of the flintlock pistol Hannah's father had insisted she learn to use and carry with her whenever she left home. This was the first time she had come close to possibly needing it. But then, what good would one gun have been against three? She blew out a heavy sigh. Perhaps she should let Michael escort her to the Reeds from now on.

five

Hannah could barely wait to get to Reed Springs to see how her stranger had fared overnight. *Dear Lord, please let him be all right.*

"Them men's lookin' fo' that stranger you done got stowed up at the Reeds, ain't they?"

Hannah stared at Chesny. The dark-skinned woman was beginning to age. More gray than black hair peeked out from her head wrap, and small wrinkles were etched in the corners of her eyes and around her mouth. She boldly held Hannah's gaze, unlike most Negroes. Hannah nodded.

"I wonder what that young feller done to rile them so."

"I don't know, but nothing could deserve such a beating. I do believe they aim to kill him." Hannah wrung her hands. "We can't let them find him, and if they're of a mind to search the Reeds' house, none of the servants would be able to stop them."

Chesny leaned forward just as Simeon pulled the buggy to a stop in front of the Reed Springs main house. "We needs to put him in the hidey hole."

Hannah jumped up and hugged her maid. "Perfect! Why didn't I think of that?"

"Because you ain't played in that place in years."

Hannah climbed down. "I'll go and check on our patient, and you can see what state the secret room is in."

Chesny clambered out of the buggy backward. On the ground, she straightened her dress and head wrap, then followed Hannah inside and up the stairs.

Hannah glanced back over her shoulder. "Why aren't you

checking on the room?"

"I ain't leavin' you and that feller all alone together."

Hannah reached the landing, shaking her head. "What's he going to do? He's stuck in bed and needs help so much as to sit up."

"He be in bed—in a nightshirt, no less. Just ain't proper for you two youngun's to be alone in a bedroom."

Hannah knew Chesny was only watching out for her and doing as Hannah's mother would do if she were here. She took a breath, then tiptoed into the room. She stopped next to the bed and watched her stranger's chest rise and fall with his steady breathing. He'd shaven—or been shaved. His wounded eye was as large as a goose egg and colored an angry black and purple. His lips were still swollen, and the bandage on his head needed changing.

She turned and tiptoed back to Chesny. "See, he's asleep, so you can go ahead and check out the secret room."

Chesny crossed her arms over her ample bosom. "I ain't goin' nowheres—leastwise not unless you go, too."

Hannah rolled her eyes and strode from the room. Downstairs in the dining room, she stopped in front of a sideboard that ofttimes when she visited as a child with her parents had been covered with food. Her hand grazed across the smooth wood of the elegantly carved sideboard, and for a moment she lost herself in the memories.

Those had been enjoyable times when she'd played with the Reed children. She'd been the youngest child. Jamie and Cooper were both older than her and Michael, though Coop was only three years her senior.

She glanced around, making sure no one other than Chesny saw her; then she crossed the room to a pantry that sat between the dining room and the stairs to the kitchen on the first floor. She reached her hand behind a large crock and found the lever that opened the door of the secret room.

She pushed on a wide board, and the door swung back. The opening was much smaller than she remembered. Glancing behind her, she caught Chesny's eye. "Do Maisy and Leta know about this room?"

Chesny nodded. "They do."

"We're going to need a lantern." Hannah studied the opening. Her stranger would have to turn sideways to get in. She hoped moving him again wouldn't be a mistake.

But then, she could hardly take a chance that those men might find him and finish the job she was certain they had started.

Back upstairs, she studied the sleeping man. His politeness and gentleness in the face of so much pain impressed her. She wondered if he had a family who worried about him. A mother and father. A special lady friend or wife. Suddenly it dawned on her there was something else she could do to help this stranger in need. She could pray.

She bowed her head. "Dear Lord, why would anyone want to hurt this man? I know a blow to the head and broken ribs can be serious. Please watch over him and heal his body. Give me wisdom to know how to treat his wounds, and if those men are after him, Lord, please don't let them find him."

❧

He awoke to the sound of ripping fabric. The young woman—Miss Madison—stood at his feet, tearing a large piece of cloth into smaller pieces.

"You came back." He smiled, stinging his lips.

"Did you think I'd forget about you?"

He shrugged. "Where is your friend?"

"She left this morning on her father's vessel, bound for Charleston."

"Ah, well, I'm glad you're here and not her."

Miss Madison's brows lifted as if in chastisement. She

turned away, but not before he caught the tiniest of smiles teasing the corners of her lips. She walked to the window and stared out. "You should not say such things."

"Why not? I'm simply speaking the truth. Your friend was obviously put off being in the same room with me, where you graciously tended my wounds with care even though you could have easily assigned one of your servants to do the task." If anyone had ever touched him so tenderly, he couldn't remember. He winced. What a shame it would be to forget something like that.

What else was he not remembering?

He stared up at the ceiling, searching the vast emptiness of his mind. How could he have lived to be a grown man but not know anything of his past?

Miss Madison's servant bustled through the door, carrying a tray. The scent of eggs and ham drifted toward him. His stomach hollered for attention. He attempted to sit up, but a sharp pain in his side shoved him back to the bed. He sucked in a ragged breath.

Miss Madison rushed to his bedside. "What's wrong?"

"Nothing."

The servant stepped to her side and scowled. "You should'a waited on me, Miz Hannah."

He eyed the woman and her servant. It seemed odd for the black woman to be talking to her mistress in such a manner, but it didn't seem to bother Miss Madison.

"Don't you think we should move him before he eats?" Miss Madison glanced at her servant.

"Move me?"

"We. . .uh. . .had an encounter with some ruffians this morning." Miss Madison wrung her hands together, her pretty face puckered with worry. "They were looking for a man who resembled you."

"Me?" Who would be after him? What had he done? He

pressed his palms against his forehead. Why couldn't he remember?

Miss Madison gently pulled his hand down. "Don't fret. It won't help things."

He glared up at her. "How would you feel if you knew nothing about who you were, not even your name? I don't know if I have a family who's worried about me or if I'm totally alone in the world. And now you say someone may be hunting for me. I may be putting you in danger by simply being in your home." He blew out a frustrated breath.

"We're prepared for that. There's a special hiding place in this home, and that's where we're moving you."

"But first, you needs to eat up and get some strength in them legs of yo's." The Negro woman set the food tray on a nearby table that held a lamp.

"Do you think you can sit up if we help you?" Miss Madison smiled, her beautiful blue eyes lighting up, and he felt he could do just about anything to make her grin again. He nodded.

"Wonderful. Chesny, if you'll reach across the bed and take hold of his right hand, I'll help lift his shoulders. Maybe we won't put too much pressure on his ribs that way."

The servant eyed him and looked as if she would argue with her mistress, but then she reached across the bed and held out her hand. Miss Madison bent down and slid an arm behind his shoulders. In spite of the older woman watching him like a mother bear, he tilted his head slightly and sniffed Miss Madison's sweet scent. Would her skin be as soft to touch as it looked?

A yank on his arm brought him back to his senses. He glanced up to meet Chesny's narrowed gaze. "You'd best hurry and eat 'fo' them men come for you."

"Are you ready?" Miss Madison's cheek was pleasingly close to his, but this time he kept his head properly facing forward.

"Yes, ma'am."

"All right then. Just take it carefully. I don't want to hurt you any more than you have already been."

Bracing for the unwanted pain he knew was coming, he took as deep a breath as was possible with his chest tied up tighter than a woman's corset. With a heave, he hoisted himself up, with one lady pushing and the other pulling. Every little movement sent pain resonating from his head to his toes. No, come to think of it, his toes were about the only part of his body that didn't hurt.

He finally sat up with his legs hanging off the side of the bed. Fighting the dizziness that made the room tilt on its axis, he closed his eyes and leaned forward. Miss Madison's firm grip on his shoulder offered him support as he struggled to regain his balance. He concentrated on a mental picture of Miss Madison's golden hair and kind blue eyes. After a few moments, he opened his eyes. The room slowly came back into focus.

The woman's steadying hand remained on his shoulder. "Are you all right now? If I let go, you won't fall, will you?"

"He ain't gonna fall, not so long as I's got ahold of him."

The servant released his hand but stood so close he could have leaned against her for support if he was of a mind to. But he wasn't. Now if that had been Miss Madison. . .

"I'm fine." He spat out the words a bit harsher than he'd planned.

"If'n you's so fine, then haul yo'self over to that table and start eatin'."

He glanced at the servant's stern glare with his one good eye and couldn't help smiling. She sure was cocky for a slave, but he liked her for it and for her protectiveness where Miss Madison was concerned. "Yes, ma'am. I'll do that, just as soon as my head stops spinning like the wheel of a ship that's lost its helmsman in a storm."

Much to his surprise, the woman's features softened. "You

ketch a lot more flies with molasses than you does with vinegar."

Miss Madison pulled the chair out from under the small table and hurried back to his side. "Do you think you've sailed on a ship before? It sure sounds like you know something about them from the analogy you used."

He stared up at her, searching the shadowy recesses of his mind. Did he know something about ships? If he did, his mind was keeping it a secret. He shrugged one shoulder. "Wish I knew."

Her bright expression dimmed. He hated disappointing her. "Well, you'll remember one of these days. I'm certain."

For now, he'd have to rely on her faith that he'd get better, because he had little of his own.

He stood and was surprised to see that the pain in his side was less severe. The scent of the food drew him to the table. He picked up the plate and stood at the window, shoveling in the delicious meal. He could almost feel the strength returning to his body.

He stared down at the manicured gardens, laden with color. Beyond them stretched a wide green lawn with a creek off to the right and a white gazebo. "You certainly have a nice home here."

"It's not actually my home. I live at Madison Gardens, which is the nearest plantation. The Reed family lives here. They've been gone for a while but will be returning soon. I'm overseeing the cleanup here. I want to make sure everything is in order when the family comes back. They suffered a tragedy of late."

He swallowed the bite of biscuit covered in sweet, creamy butter; then he took a swig of his coffee and glanced at her. "I'm sorry."

She smiled up at him, her eyes sad. He wondered what had happened but didn't feel it was his place to ask. He scraped the plate and shoved the last bite into his mouth. How long had it been since he'd tasted anything so good? "My compliments to the cook."

Chesny nodded. "I'll let Leta know you enjoyed her cookin'."

"So, where's this clandestine room?" He didn't like the idea of hiding, but if keeping his presence secret would ensure the women's safety, he'd cooperate.

"Downstairs. If you're ready, we'll help you."

"I think I can get there on my own. Just show me the way."

Chesny picked up the tray of food and carried it toward the door. She shook her head, cast a glance back at him, and he thought he heard her mutter something about stubborn men. Alone again with Miss Madison, he gazed down at her. Wispy curls as golden as corn silk. Deep blue eyes that rivaled the color of the ocean on a sunny day. And skin so creamy that his fingers ached to touch it.

She nibbled on her lower lip in an intriguing manner that stirred his senses. He swallowed hard.

"Are you certain you're up to walking on your own?"

He was most likely a fool to refuse her assistance, knowing that meant he could put his arm around her and hold her close to his side, but he wanted her to see him as a man and not just her patient. "I'll be fine."

"All right, but if you start getting faint, let me know, and I'll help you."

He was getting weaker already, but he wasn't sure if it was from being on his feet so soon after receiving his wounds or because of her nearness. He nodded, pushed away from the wall, and walked across the room. His head swirled, and the doorway blurred into two. He grabbed hold of the door frame to steady himself.

Miss Madison hurried to his side. "Do you need to sit for a moment?"

He shook his head, immediately sorry. Summoning up all the strength left in his body, he held one arm against his side and angled for the stairway across the wide parlor. He made it to the railing and gazed down the cavern of steps. The wide opening darkened then came back into focus. His breakfast threatened to escape from his belly.

Miss Madison stepped to his side. "If you don't mind, I'd feel better helping you downstairs. Head wounds like yours can cause dizziness, and the last thing you need is to stumble and fall down the stairs."

As much as he hated admitting it, he needed her help. And since he did, he might as well enjoy the moment. He nodded. She paused and stared up at him, as if unsure now about touching him.

He offered a smile to calm her nerves. "It's all right. I don't bite—at least I don't believe I do."

She grinned and stepped closer. "I'm glad to know that. I was very worried."

She placed her arm around his waist and his arm encircled her shoulders, which seemed far too thin to support his weight. He leaned against the stair railing as much as possible, and with her next to him, the journey down was not all unpleasant.

But when she showed him the door to the secret room, he balked. The small, dark opening reminded him of another place he'd been, but he couldn't quite grab hold of the image in his mind. All he knew was that it wasn't a good place. And it had rats. He pressed his hand on the door frame and refused to go farther. "I—I can't go in there."

Miss Madison gazed up at him, her chin almost resting against his chest. "Why not? It's just a room. The opening is a bit dark, but there's a lantern once you get around the corner."

His whole body trembled. The memory screamed for release,

but the door of his mind kept it locked away. Maybe one day soon he'd locate the key. He closed his eyes. If he remained outside of the room and those men came, he—and the women—could get hurt. He was in no shape to protect them, other than to point a flintlock at someone. The best thing he could do was disappear—and going into the room was his only option for the moment. *Help me, Lord.*

"It's all right. I'll stay with you until you're comfortable. It's really a nice-sized room."

He huffed out a laugh. "It's idiotic, is it not? A man afraid of the dark."

"No, it's not." She tightened her grip around his waist. "You don't know the source of your fear. I'm sure there's a perfectly logical reason you don't want to go in there."

Perhaps she was right. But even if she was, he needed to conquer his fear and face the room.

A loud pounding on the front door made Miss Madison jump. Her eyes widened. "What if it's those men?"

He clenched his jaw and stared into the shadows. A ghost of light danced at the edge of the darkness. He would concentrate on that—reaching the light. Forcing one foot forward, he heard quick footsteps behind him.

"Git yo'self in that room and shut the door. I'll go see who's making all that ruckus out front." Chesny scurried behind him and Miss Madison.

With each shaky step he took into the room, the light grew stronger. He turned the corner and discovered a stairway that led down to a room about six feet long and four feet wide. He swallowed back the bile burning his throat. Smaller than he'd hoped for, but at least the bright lantern illuminated the area with flickers of dancing light on the walls and ceiling.

A narrow cot lined one wall. A table holding the lantern and a pitcher of water and two chairs filled the other wall. A shelf on the far end held a half dozen books and some jars of food. He made for the nearest chair and collapsed into it. He already missed the warmth of the sun shining in the window.

Miss Madison hurried away and shut the door. He thought she'd locked him in, but then he heard the rustle of her dress, and relief washed over him. He could face this if he wasn't alone. But he'd been alone for a long while now, hadn't he?

"Don't look so glum." She squeezed past him and sat in the other chair. "Maybe once those men stop by and don't find you, they'll move on."

He shook his head. "We can't take that chance. I sense they *are* after me, as you said, but I have no clue as to why."

He leaned his elbows on the table and rested his head in his hands. Suddenly, it dawned on him that he'd asked God's help to face his fears. Perhaps God would also heal his mind.

six

One man held his shoulders while another man kicked him, over and over, yelling something about some papers. The vision of a woman and man, their faces hidden by shadows, floated across the dark chasm of his mind. There was something familiar about them, and he reached out. Just when they drew close enough that he could almost see their faces, they drifted away again.

Food now. A platter heaping with fried chicken glided into the space the couple had vacated. No. Maybe he actually smelled *real* food. The fogginess of sleep ebbed, but he couldn't quite tell if he was awake or dreaming. He blinked his heavy eyelids and forced them to stay open. Flickers of light sashayed across the walls and low ceiling. His eyes closed again.

A low, rumbling snarl forced its way into his stupor. Suddenly he jerked wide awake and focused on the teeth of a wolf-like creature, standing at the bottom of the stairs. Ignoring the pain clawing at his chest, he scrambled back against the far wall, distancing himself from the creature's hair-raising growl. He blinked again. Was this real or just another nightmare?

Someone at the table moved, and he realized Hannah was still there. She set aside something she was stitching and reached out and tapped the dreadful creature on its snout, effectively silencing it.

"I'm sorry that Buster frightened you. He wandered over from Madison Gardens. One of our workers came over to check on us, and I thought it was a good idea for you to meet him with me present. He can be quite nasty if he happens to cross your path and he doesn't know you." She reached her hand toward him. "If you feed Buster this bit of meat, he'll take a shine to you. His bark is much worse than his bite."

"I don't believe that for a moment." He studied the somewhat calmer beast, then glanced back at Hannah's face. Her warm smile encouraged him. With more than a little trepidation, he took the chunk of chicken from her hand, just as the beast growled again.

"Hush, Buster. This man's our friend. This is Adam."

He jerked his gaze back to Miss Madison. "Adam? That's my name? How did you discover it?"

"I didn't. I made it up. I decided that we need to have something to call you." Her cheeks turned deep red in the glow of the lantern, and she shrugged. "Since you're the first man, except for Israel and Simeon, of course, to come to Reed Springs in ages, and it seems you may have a broken rib or two, I figured it's a good name for you. You do know the first man mentioned in God's Holy Book was named Adam, don't you?"

He nodded his head. The name sounded familiar even though he couldn't remember the story. "I suppose Adam works all right, at least until I remember my real name."

Adam pushed against the wall and managed to sit up. "Come here, Buster." He held the meat out to the beast, wondering if he'd have all his fingers afterward. Based on the stature of the beast standing at the foot of the bed, he felt he had every right to be a bit nervous, but the last thing he wanted was for Hannah to think he was lily-livered.

Adam—the name was growing on him—leaned forward, holding out the meat. The wolf-like animal's gray-and-black head popped up, and he snarled a low, menacing growl. Adam held his breath while the big dog crept toward him. The vicious-looking snout sniffed his hand. Grayish-black ears twitched forward and back, and beady onyx eyes stared him down. Sweat trickled down Adam's temple, but he didn't move an inch. The brute's wet nose touched his hand, and sharp yellow teeth clicked together as the dog cocked its head and snatched the morsel away. Buster gave Adam a final sniff, turned, and trod back up the steps.

"Guess I passed muster, huh?"

"That wasn't so bad, was it?"

He stared at her but didn't comment. Anything he said would make him sound less masculine.

"Do you feel like eating something yourself?"

He reached up, wiping the drops of sweat from his temple. He hoped she hadn't noticed his discomfort. "I swear I've been dreaming about fried chicken. I can even smell it."

Hannah's gentle laughter rippled through the small room. "You're smelling chicken all right, but it's soup, not fried. It's been there on your table for fifteen minutes while I went back upstairs for some blankets. Do you feel like sitting at the table for a while?"

Adam nodded and pushed up from the bed. The simple effort of moving sent daggers of pain radiating throughout his head and chest, but once he was upright, the pain lessened. Leaning back against the wall, he studied Hannah as she scooped up a spoon of soup and held it out to him. His lips tugged into a smile. "If I'd have known I was going to be spoon-fed by such a lovely lady, I'd have stayed abed."

She smiled and lowered her eyes and the spoon. "My apologies. I don't want to baby you, but I also don't want you overdoing things and being sorry later."

He lowered himself into the chair, taking care to keep his torso rigid. He breathed in the delicious scent of the chicken soup, but it was the bowl that snagged his attention the most. Running his finger around the indigo-and-white, rope-like scroll, he grasped at ethereal memories drifting through the haze of his mind. He picked up the bowl and cocked his head, studying the small red flowers clustered against a bed of green leaves.

Hannah leaned forward. The glow of the lantern was reflected in her blue eyes—eyes as deep a blue as the indigo design on the bowl. "Do you recognize that pattern?"

He scrunched his eyes together, grappling for a hold. The memory was there, but the fingers of his mind couldn't latch on to it. Sighing, he set the bowl down. "Perhaps." He flung his hand in the air. "I don't know. I thought it seemed familiar."

Hannah reached across the narrow table. "You realize you've seen this design somewhere, but just can't remember where. That tells me the memories are there and will be revealed soon, but you've got to allow your wounds time to heal." She pulled back her hand and touched the plate holding a half dozen slices of bread. "This is an English pattern that's been in the Reed family for generations. Do you think you might have been in England before?"

He shrugged. "Who knows? I could have been anywhere, for all I know." Hating the self-pity in his voice, he grabbed a slice of bread and dunked it into the soup. The amazing flavors of the soft bread and salty soup teased his tongue. It had been a long time since he'd eaten food this fresh.

The food was delicious, and he devoured it, but what he enjoyed most was the close-up view of his rescuer. Tight spirals of blond hair hung down the sides of Hannah's face where they'd pulled loose from her mobcap. Shorter wisps curled across her forehead in an enticing manner. He wanted to reach out and touch one, but he kept his hands flat against the table.

A sudden thought drew his gaze back to the last of his food. *Do I have a woman somewhere waiting for me to return?*

❧

Hannah sat stiffly in the chair, trying not to stare at her patient. Last night, she had dreamed about him. And today, she kept getting the feeling she'd seen him before. But was that simply because she was getting more familiar with him?

He would be a handsome man when his wounds healed. His injured eye was slightly open today, but it was still purple. The cut on his lip looked better, but more bruises had appeared on his face. He sure didn't complain much. If Michael were in his shoes, he'd be soaking up the pampering and demanding more.

Though she knew little about Adam, she liked him for some reason she couldn't explain.

Footsteps sounded, and then Chesny stopped on the landing. "That boy down there behavin' hisself?"

"Yes, ma'am. I am. And thanks for this delicious food. I'm going to be spoiled with all this caring attention I'm getting." He held up his cup of coffee as if in toast to Chesny.

"Ah, you do go on. If'n you needs mo' food, I can fetch you some." Chesny scooted sideways between the table and the cot. She gathered the empty dishes. "You want some mo' soup?"

Adam leaned back stiffly in the chair and patted his stomach. "No, thank you, but it was most tasty."

Chesny beamed. "I like a man that know what's good and is grateful fo' it." She trod back up the stairs, humming a tune.

Adam leaned forward. "Why is she leaving us alone?"

Hannah had wondered the same thing. "I don't know except that she must not see you as a threat any longer."

"Good." He tapped the table. "I'm not a danger to any of you. You said this is not your home." Adam swiped his hand through the air. "So tell me about where you do live. It must be nearby since you can go back and forth daily."

"It is. Just a little over a mile. I live on a plantation called Madison Gardens with my parents, Richard and Caroline Madison, and my older brother, Michael. We also have a home in Charleston, where my father has an import/export business, although I tend to stay at the plantation far more than I do the town house."

"Why is that? Seems like a pretty, young woman would want to be closer to her friends and closer to town events like parties and concerts."

Hannah shook her head. "I've always loved living on the estate. Town is noisy and it smells. I do enjoy a party now and then, but not several in a single week like people often have in Charleston."

He nodded. Hannah wondered if he had been to Charleston and knew what she meant, but she kept quiet. If he didn't remember, she didn't want to bring that to mind again. She couldn't imagine how horrible it must be to not remember your family or friends.

"So what's this place? Why do you come here since you don't live here?"

"The barn I found you in belongs to my parents' oldest and dearest friends. Lucas and Heather Reed had two sons that were somewhat close in age to Michael and me. Jamie is older than Cooper by six years, Cooper is just a year older than Michael, and three years older than me." But there were things she couldn't say. Didn't want to say. Such as explaining that Jamie was her fiancé. Or that Cooper was probably dead by now. Still, there were happier times she could tell about. "I remember their dark hair and mischievous grins."

"So are they living in Charleston now?"

Hannah's heart leaped. "Uh. . .no. They're on a trip to England."

Adam scowled and looked lost in thought. What did a person with no memories think about?

"England sounds very familiar. I surely must have been there a time or two."

"It sounds to me like you have a bit of an English accent."

His gaze snapped up and caught hers. "Truly? Do you think so?"

"Perhaps a little, but I doubt that you're from there or your accent would be thicker. With all the tensions between England and America now, it's probably a good thing if you aren't."

He drummed his fingertips on the table and yawned. "What tensions?"

Hannah pressed her lips together, unsure just how much to say. What if he turned out to be a British spy, after all? Could she be endangering her family by talking about the struggles their young nation was still having with England?

She stared at him and somehow deep within knew he could be trusted. She couldn't have explained it to anyone, but she just knew. "There's talk that there may be another war between England and America."

"*Another* war?" His perplexed expression tugged at her heart, but suddenly his countenance brightened. "Yes. We did fight a war—for our independence. Isn't that correct?"

She nodded and smiled. "Yes. And there are Englishmen who still think it a travesty that the lowly colonists were able to defeat mighty Britain." She stood and paced the small area, nearly touching him as she passed by. She'd listened to her father and his friends debate the pros and cons of another conflict with England numerous times.

"England is refusing to trade with American shippers. But the worst thing is that, because Britain lost so many young men during the years of the Revolution and then still others who abdicated to America, they are short sailors for their own ships. They are capturing *our* ships and forcing *our* sailors into service for the king. It's atrocious."

She paced to the stairs and turned back. Adam's elbows rested on the table and his fingers were forked through his dark hair. He glanced up, and all the color had run from his face. She hurried to his side. "I think you need to lie down."

"No." He shot out of the chair then grimaced and grabbed his side. "I—I think I may have been on one of those ships."

She opened her mouth to question him, but a scream upstairs silenced her. She spun around and hurried to the top of the stairs. Adam was right behind her. Hannah lifted her foot to step out of the room, but Adam yanked her back against him and closed the door, leaving only an inch open.

She turned in his arms, ready to scold him. Something was going on, and the servants needed her.

The light from the room illuminated one side of his face, and he held a finger to his lips. "Shh. . ."

Hannah forced herself to stand still and listen, but all she heard was the sound of her pounding heart. Adam's hand still rested across her mouth, but gently, not hurting. His hand was warm against her lips.

A deep voice growled. Glass shattered. Hannah jumped. Adam slid his arm from her mouth, wrapped it around her shoulders, and pulled her against his chest.

She could no longer breathe. Never had she been held in such a manner by a man, other than by her father.

"Where is he? And where is that pretty lady?"

"Nowheres, suh."

Hannah recognized Leta's terrified voice.

Another crash of glass rent the air. "Don't lie to me. Where is that Madison gal? I seen her come over in that buggy this morning."

"I—I don't know, suh. I think she done returned back to her home, I th–think."

"Check the other rooms."

Hannah stiffened at the sound of Boss's voice. Heavy footsteps thudded across the floor in different directions. So, they'd actually come, and if she hadn't moved Adam to the secret room, they would have found him. *Thank You, Lord, for protecting Adam. Please keep the others safe, too.*

Adam quietly closed the door the rest of the way, plunging them into darkness. His warm breath tickled her cheek.

She stepped back, but her spine connected with the wall.

"Let's stay right here. We don't want to chance the stairs squeaking and giving us away." His soft whispers teased her ear, sending her stomach into spasms.

"I—"

"Shhh. . .no talking." Adam's hand found her mouth again, but instead of covering it, he ran his finger across her lower lip, effectively stealing away her breath, her thoughts, and any words she might utter. Her heart thrummed in a way it never had when Jamie was near. He was always gentle and considerate, but he'd never touched her in such a provocative manner, as if she were someone special. He'd never even kissed her. Yes, he was a good friend, but was friendship enough to build a marriage on?

seven

Buster's low-pitched growl yanked Hannah back to the events at hand. Footsteps came in their direction, and a man cried out. Buster's fierce snarls nearly drowned out the man's frantic howls. She wanted to jerk open the door and help her dog, but she didn't dare. Surely the men would leave if they didn't find what they wanted.

A gun exploded on the other side of the wall, and Hannah jumped. Buster yelped; then things grew eerily quiet. Adam tightened his grip around her, as if cradling her from the danger. Tears stung her eyes. Had they shot her dog?

Scuffling sounded just outside the hidden door. She wanted to run out and check on Chesny and the other workers. She wanted to see if Buster was hurt and needed tending. She wanted to stay just where she was, nestled in Adam's arms.

Thumps and thuds echoed from the other side of the wall. Someone muttered a curse. For long minutes all she heard was the sound of Adam's breath, his heartbeat, and a ringing in her ears from straining to hear what was happening outside their cocoon.

She prayed for each of the workers and for Buster. *Don't let those men harm them.*

Adam's grip on her lessened, and he backed down the first step, putting a gap between them. She touched her warm cheeks, suddenly embarrassed by her behavior. What was she doing clinging to Adam like that?

She crossed her arms. Yes, she'd been afraid. All her life she'd lived a quiet, fairly sheltered life and had never encountered bad men bent on hurting someone before. Both her parents were loving, kindhearted people. She wished her father or Michael had been present to chase those men away, but she would have to be the strong one today if things had gone bad on the other side of the wall. One day soon she'd be mistress of this plantation, and she had to have gumption and grit to keep it running. Things wouldn't always go smoothly.

She stiffened at the sound of hurried footsteps. The door rattled, and Adam reached out and squeezed her hand, then stepped up in front of her. She peered around his arm. Either they were caught or someone had come to inform them of the situation.

Chesny appeared as the door fell back. "Is you two all right in here?"

"Us?" Hannah shoved Adam back against the wall and squeezed past him. "Is everyone safe? Is Buster hurt bad?"

"We's all fine. Israel took that beast of yo's out to the barn. He was winged, but not too bad. Them men's gone, so you can come out if'n you wants."

Hannah slipped past Chesny. Spots of blood still pooled on the wooden floor. She glanced at her maid.

"Some of that belongs to that dog and some of it to the scoundrel he bit." She looked up at Adam. "They's looking fo' you, from the sound of it. What'd you do?"

Adam glanced past her to Hannah and leaned against the doorjamb. He looked exhausted. "I wish I knew."

"Where's Maisy and Leta?" Hannah asked.

"Maisy's upstairs straightening what them men messed up when they's searching fo' him. Leta's out helpin' Israel."

"I need to check on Buster. Could you clean this up?" Hannah motioned to the blood.

Chesny nodded. "That's just what I was fixin' to do." She bustled to the back of the house and disappeared around the corner.

Hannah stepped closer to Adam. "You should go lie down and rest."

"I should do something to help."

She shook her head. "It's too soon. You took a fierce clobbering, and you need to regain your strength. Besides, those men might still be keeping watch on the house. If they see you outside or through one of the windows, they'll come back, and next time they might not let you live." She didn't want to mention that the men might also not be too happy that Chesny and the others had lied to them.

Adam blew out a heavy sigh. "All right, but when I'm better, I want to do something around here to help out. I'm used to pulling my own weight—not taking charity."

Hannah lifted her chin. "It's not charity to save a man's life."

"I just don't like hiding behind a bunch of women's skirts or being in that cave." He motioned toward the secret room.

"Well, those *skirts* and that *cave* may have just saved your life for a second time."

He held her gaze for a long moment, then turned and ambled back down the stairs. She watched for a moment and shut the door. She supposed she wouldn't like being stuck in the hole alone either, but he could at least show a little gratitude.

She spun away, determined to check on her dog and put the mysterious stranger from her mind, but with each step she took, his scent traveled with her. The feel of his arms around her warmed her from the inside out. Would hugging Jamie feel as. . .wonderful?

As much as she wished it were so, she didn't think it would.

❧

Adam trod down the stairs, back into his dark pit. The dank, dreary hole reminded him of another place—not a good place—but he couldn't latch on to where that place was. Weary beyond belief, he stopped at the table and downed the last of the chilled coffee. He set the mug down and started to turn away when Hannah's stitching caught his eye.

He swiped his hands on his pants, then picked up the ecru fabric and held it up to the light. The sampler had an intricate, scrolling, ivy and floral border on three sides. At the bottom was a house resembling the three-story, redbrick home he was staying in, surrounded by trees and more flowers. Could the houses be one and the same?

Above the house, Hannah had expertly stitched a Bible verse: "If a Man Say, I Love God, and Hateth His Brother, He Is a Liar: For He That Loveth Not His Brother Whom He Hath Seen, How Can He Love God Whom He Hath Not Seen?" 1 John 4:20.

Below the verse in larger cursive letters was the saying, Next to God, Family Is. . .

He blew out a breath and set the unfinished stitchwork on the table. Whom was she making the sampler for? Her parents? A friend who was getting married?

Holding his side, he slowly lowered himself to the cot and lay down. With his arm behind his head, he closed his eyes. He ought to be helping set things in order upstairs, but the truth of the matter was he felt like an eighty-year-old man. His head pounded in a steady rhythm. He pressed his fingertips into the indentation just above his neck and massaged it, receiving some relief. He yawned.

Next to God, family is. . .

What?

Next to God, family is. . .

Most important.

Adam's eyes shot open. Next to God, family is most important.

How could he possibly know what Hannah's sampler would say? Was his mind just searching for words that fit? If so, why had those particular ones come to mind?

He had heard them before. He knew them in the core of his being. Adam thumped his chest. He didn't know his real name or where he was from. He didn't know who his parents were or if he was married, but in his heart, he knew those words.

"Next to God, family is most important."

♠

Hannah walked toward the barn, struggling to get her wayward thoughts under control, and concentrated on thinking positive things about Jamie. The Reed boys had been good friends as children. She'd played more with Cooper because he was closer to Michael and her in age, but she would soon be marrying Jamie.

She hadn't seen him since he was home for Christmas. He'd gone back to Charleston, to his work at the Reed shipping yard, with the promise to return a few weeks before the wedding, but when word came that Cooper was missing, they hopped one of his father's clipper ships and went to England. Would Jamie return in time or would the wedding have to be postponed?

She couldn't help wondering how England's embargo against American products had hurt his business. She supposed he could still build ships, but fewer people would want to purchase them if they were unable to sail them without fear of them being confiscated by His Majesty's navy.

A high-pitched whine drew her back to the task at hand. She slipped through the open barn door and searched for Israel. Maisy stood leaning against one of the stalls, and she found Israel on his knees, stitching up Buster's hip. The dog gazed up with pain-filled eyes and whined. Hannah hurried to his side.

"Don't you be movin' none, dog. I know it hurts," Israel said.

"Oh, you poor thing." Hannah dropped down into the straw, heedless of her dress.

Maisy straightened. "Oh Miz Hannah, let me fetch you a blanket to sit on."

She waved her hand. "Thank you, but I'm fine. Buster may have well saved some of our lives today. The least I can do is comfort him."

"You's a good woman. Dat Jamie lad is lucky to be marryin' you."

Hannah forced a smile. "Thank you."

Ever since she was little, her mother had planned for her to marry Jamie. Arranged marriages were a tradition among her mother's ancestors, so her mother had said. Why had Hannah never questioned her upcoming marriage before Adam came along?

She heaved a sigh, and Buster licked her hand. She smiled, petting the dog's head. Wistful thinking wouldn't change anything. Jamie was coming back soon, and they'd be getting married. He was a good man who would provide for her well, and he had a strong belief in God.

Israel snipped the silk thread and sat back. He patted Buster's side, then reached for a bottle of whiskey and poured some over the wound. Buster yelped and snapped at the man, but then the dog licked Israel's hand.

The caretaker chuckled. "Dat dog, he knows I'ma just tryin' to help him."

Israel stood and pressed his hand to his back. "He be fine in a few days, Miz Hannah."

"Thank you so much for tending to him."

Israel nodded, then shuffled to the stall gate. He glanced at Maisy. "Could you give me and Miz Hannah a minute alone?"

Maisy's gaze shot to Hannah, but she nodded and hurried

from the barn. Hannah patted Buster's head again and stood. "Is something wrong?"

Israel rubbed his chin and rocked from foot to foot. The man had worked on the Reeds' estate for as long as she could remember. That the Reeds left him in charge when they were gone spoke a lot about the quiet man's character.

"Meb'be it's just an ol' black man's foolishness, but they's somethin' familiar about dat patient of yours. I keep gettin' a feeling in my gut dat I's seen him 'afore."

Hannah rushed forward. "Me, too! But I can't for the life of me figure out who he is. Do you think he did something bad since those men are after him?"

Israel looked deep in thought for a moment, then shook his head. "No, Miz Hannah. I don't. Dem men's what came after him is bad men, so that says to me our stranger, he must be a good man."

Hannah leaned her arms on the stall gate. "But what if he was part of their gang and stole from them? That could be why they're after him. Or perhaps he was a witness to a crime."

Her thoughts ran rampant again. She didn't want to think badly of Adam, but she had to keep her mind open to all possibilities.

Instantly, shame surged through her. How could she think badly of a man who was so gentle and polite? A man who stirred her and made her dream things an engaged woman had no business dreaming?

Israel shrugged. "I'll keep a'thinkin' on it, and meb'be it'll come to me."

Hannah peeked back at Buster. The dog was asleep with his head across his paws. "Please, Lord, heal Buster."

She closed the gate, hoping to keep the dog corralled long enough that he'd heal well; then she strode out of the barn.

She peered up at the beautiful blue sky. Soft clouds floated like tufts of cotton in the air at harvesttime. How could things be so peaceful after the morning's events?

Her feet headed for the house, but at the last minute, she turned and walked out to the garden. Spring flowers in a multitude of colors surrounded her and teased her nose with their sweet scents as she strolled the stone path. Her eyes gravitated to her favorites—the azaleas in pink, red, and white blossoms that covered their shrubs at the far end of the garden; an arched trellis blanketed with wisteria, the vivid purple clusters of flowers hanging from the arch reminding her of grapes. She sat on the bench under the arch and breathed in a deep breath.

She arranged her skirts to cover her ankles and peered up at the sky again through the canopy of flowers. Yellow butterflies flittered around the spectacular blooms. "What do I do, Lord? Why am I suddenly questioning my marriage to Jamie when I've never done so before?"

Her thoughts shot to Adam. Could God have sent him there to show her that her feelings could be so easily swayed? Was she a wanton woman to be engaged to one man and attracted to another?

She buried her face in her hands. "I don't know what to do, Lord. Reveal Your will to me. Please, Lord."

eight

"King me!" Hannah ordered, unable to hold back a victorious grin. "That's two kings for me and only one for you." Perhaps two days of playing checkers with Adam had finally improved her ability.

He grinned. "I'm not too worried. You don't exactly have an intimidating record so far. What is it? Twelve to nothing, I believe?"

Hannah glanced across the table. The smug, lopsided smile gracing Adam's face only heightened her desire to win this game. "I do believe it's your turn, *sir*."

After a few moments of studying the board for her next move, Hannah began to wonder why Adam was taking so long to make his. Usually he moved his man right on the heels of hers. She looked up to find him staring at her, and her heart turned a flip. Adam's compelling gaze captured hers.

"Do you have any idea how beautiful your eyes are?" he said, after a moment.

Hannah blinked. She opened her mouth to respond, but her shocked brain refused to communicate with her mouth. Like a driver who'd lost hold of the reins and let the horses run free, she struggled to regain control of her addled brain.

Adam glanced down, and his hand snaked out, obviously taking full advantage of her bewilderment. *Plop! Plop! Plop!* He jumped three of her men, including one of her kings. A triumphant gleam danced in his good eye. "Not too shabby for a one-eyed sick man. Huh?"

"You beast!" Hannah smacked the table, causing the remaining pieces to dance in place on the board. "No fair distracting me. Perhaps I should blacken your other eye so I'll have a fairer advantage." Hannah leaned back in her chair and crossed her arms to avoid the temptation. Losing so many games to him brought out a competitive side of her she never knew existed—and she didn't like it.

"Aw, come on, Miss Madison, you don't really think I'm a beast, do you? I can't help it if I'm a good draught player." Amusement flickered in the gaze that met hers. After a moment, Adam's grin faded as he reached behind his neck and rubbed it. He twisted his head from side to side as if he were trying to shake out the kinks.

Hannah's eyes narrowed, and she wondered if this was another ploy to distract her. She enjoyed sparring with Adam as much as he seemed to enjoy it. She pushed her last king forward and Adam immediately countered. Placing her elbow on the table, she leaned her cheek against her palm.

"Why is it you're so good at checkers, anyway?"

"Well, that's the strange thing. I can remember how to play draughts, but I can't tell you where I learned to play the game or who I played with before."

"And why do you call it *draughts*? Isn't that what the game is called in England?"

He glanced up and to the side, a movement she knew meant he was trying to remember something. He winced and ducked his head, then began massaging his forehead with his fingertips. Leaning forward with his elbows resting on the table, Adam laid his face in his hands.

"Are you still getting headaches?"

"Yeah, but mostly only when I try hard to remember things."

"Don't worry about it, Adam. I'm sure it will all come back in God's timing." She couldn't imagine what it would feel like to be totally alone, dependent on strangers, and unable to remember her family or where her home was. Family was so important, especially when you lived on an isolated plantation. How could she bear it if she couldn't see her family frequently. The only time she was separated from them was when her parents went to Charleston and she chose to stay at home on the plantation.

Perhaps that's why she accepted marriage to Jamie so easily. At least she'd always be close to home.

Not so good of a reason to get married. She stood, and Adam shot up from his chair. Hannah walked around the table, stopping beside him. "Whenever Michael or I have a headache, we massage one another's necks. May I try and see if it will help your headache?"

He stared down, his eyes holding a special look that he reserved only for her. As usual, it stole her breath away. He stared at her for a moment, then nodded and sat down again. He laid his face against his arm on the table. Hannah gently kneaded her fingertips into his shoulders and then up the back of his neck for a few minutes. "Perhaps we should call it quits for a while? What do you think?"

"Aw, you're just afraid you're going to lose—again."

She smiled at the playful tease in his voice.

"I'm worried that you're overdoin' it. You should be resting more." She continued to massage his neck and solid shoulders. Her fingers splayed through the long, dark hair draping his neck. *Such nice thick hair he has.*

"I'm tired of resting. I need to be up and moving around. Two days of being in bed is making me stiff."

"I have an idea. Why don't you lie down and rest your head a bit, and I'll read another chapter of *Robinson Crusoe*. And if you behave, perhaps I could ask Israel to take you outside for a short walk after the sun sets. How does that sound?"

Hannah stopped rubbing as Adam lifted his head and turned around in his chair to look at her. Grimacing, he grabbed his side and turned back around.

"Careful now. You shouldn't be twisting your body like that until your ribs heal."

Adam used both hands to slowly push himself up. He exhaled a loud breath. "I feel like an old man."

You sure don't look like an old man, she wanted to say, but she kept silent. "Uh—you'll be feeling better in a few more days." She reached out to help him back to the cot and looked up into his face. His tender expression took her breath away, and she thought her knees would surely give out any second.

He turned toward her and slowly reached out, cupping her cheek with his hand. If she had a breath left before, it was definitely gone now. "Hannah, I can't say I'm thankful for the attack on me, but I did meet you as a result of it, and for that, I'll be forever grateful. You've been such an encouragement to me. You know you saved my life, most likely."

Hannah stood mesmerized. He'd never used her Christian name before, and she loved the sound of it on his lips. Adam's gaze roamed her face, and she felt her cheeks flame when it rested on her lips. Goodness! He looked as if he wanted to kiss her. What would she do if he did? *Oh dear Lord, I actually think I want him to. Forgive me, Father.*

Guilt instantly assailed her, and a heaviness centered in her chest. She broke his gaze and ducked her head. *How can I be standing here wishing Adam would kiss me when I know good and well that I'm going to be married to another man soon? It's just plain improper.* No wonder Chesny didn't want them to be alone.

She opened her eyes in time to catch a brief look of disappointment flash across Adam's face. A solemn mask of reserve replaced the tenderness that had just permeated it. He ran his fingers along her jaw, and his hand dropped listlessly to his side. Hannah felt as if he'd read her thoughts. Somehow she had to tread very carefully until Adam was well enough to leave. She couldn't lose her heart to this man who'd already become her closest friend. The thought of him one day walking out of her life for good brought her more than a small measure of anxiety.

"I'll take you up on that reading, if you don't mind." Adam walked over to the cot and slowly sat down. He let out a deep sigh and leaned back against the wall with his eyes closed.

Hannah watched him for a moment, wondering what was going through his mind. Did he interpret her distancing herself from him as not caring?

She moved over to the table and turned up the lamp. The dimmer lighting was all right for playing a board game, but not for reading. She glanced up the stairs, wondering what time it was. It wouldn't be good to head for home after darkness set in. Things would be much easier if Chesny would allow her to stay the night at Reed Springs while she cared for Adam, but the woman flat refused to budge on that issue.

Hannah tugged the book off the shelf on the wall and sat in the chair Adam had vacated. She would read quickly.

❧

Adam reached up to touch his ear, which he was certain must be beet red. *What a fool I am! I actually wanted to kiss Hannah.*

He knew she was only doing her Christian duty to aid a stranger in need. Yet he couldn't deny his overwhelming attraction to her. Was it wrong for him to be so drawn to her? She was compassionate, gentle, and pretty. But he was fooling himself to believe a woman like her could actually fall for a man who didn't even know his own name.

Wrestling with his confusion, his heart wrenched at the memory of Hannah's expression moments earlier. Her fingers biting into his neck, massaging the tenseness out, had felt like a little piece of heaven. She had encouraged him and looked as if she couldn't tear her eyes away from his. He mistakenly thought she actually wanted him to kiss her.

Then suddenly, a look of sheer panic engulfed her face. Women were so hard to decipher.

Adam jumped at the sound of the book slamming shut. With remorse, he realized he hadn't heard a single word Hannah had just read.

"Sorry. I didn't mean to startle you. Were you sleeping?"

"No, just resting."

"It's time I was going. We need to get home before the sun sets."

"What about the walk you promised me? I could do with a heavy dose of sunshine. Besides Maisy or Israel, you're the only other living creature I see all day. You also said you'd tell me about your family and your plantation."

Hannah laid the book on the table and smoothed her skirt. "I suppose I could be persuaded to stay a short while longer. What is it you want to know about my family?"

"I don't know." Adam rubbed his hand along his whiskery chin, creating a bristly noise. "Umm, how long have you lived on. . .what is it called?"

She smiled, and a butterfly danced in Adam's belly. "Madison Gardens. I guess you'd have to say I've lived there my whole life, except for our regular treks to Charleston. I was born on the plantation."

"Guess it's in your blood then. You just have one brother and no sisters?"

"No, actually I also have an older brother and sister, Kit and Jane. My father and Lucas Reed found them in the woods before Michael was born and adopted them. Jane's married, and Kit is off sailing on one of our father's ships, so Michael is the only one still at home. He's a great brother— don't take me wrong. I love him, but he's such a tease."

"Must be nice to have such a large family. Didn't you mention being friends with the people who live here?"

Hannah nodded. "Jamie and Cooper Reed. Our families

visited one another quite often when I was young. We still do, in fact."

Jamie. That name sounded strangely familiar. "I remember you told me about them the other day, when you were doctoring me, I believe." He reached up and tugged on the bandage around his head.

"They're the family who used to live here. Jamie, the oldest son, and Kit were always playin' tricks on Coop, Michael, and me. It used to make me so mad."

Adam's eyes narrowed. *Jamie.* She'd mentioned that name several times now, and he'd begun to notice an odd look in her expression that wasn't there when she talked about the others. Was there more to their relationship than just friendship? He definitely needed to pry more information out of her concerning this Jamie fellow.

Adam sat up. "So, tell me more about Jamie and—what's his brother's name?"

"Jamie and Cooper. I played with them from the time I could sit up. But like I said, Michael and I mostly played with Cooper and helped him with his chores."

"So you never ran around with Jamie?"

Hannah gave him a curious stare. "Well, certainly. From the stories my parents tell, Jamie was quite enamored with me when I was younger and would carry me around. Our families did many things together, for one reason or another, mainly because they're our closest neighbors." She cocked her head. "Why did you want to know?"

"Just curious, I suppose." He felt the need to change the subject before his curiosity got him in trouble. "Have your parents always lived here?" He flicked a fly off his leg. "Surely, you get together with your other neighbors at times. Don't you?" The fly buzzed his face. He swatted his hand in the air to shoo it away and inwardly sighed when it flew up the stairway. "Why is your slave so bossy?"

Hannah straightened; her lips puckered. "Slavery is abominable. The Madisons do not own slaves, and neither do the Reeds. Our workers are employees who are paid a salary and treated as all humans deserve to be."

He held up one palm. "My apologies. I wasn't aware of that, but it is an admirable stand to take, and one I'm sure is not overly popular among most Southerners."

She deflated as quickly as a hen drenched in a downpour. Hannah sighed. "That's true, and probably the reason I don't have more friends."

"Is that partly the reason you stay on the plantation when most women your age would much prefer to be in Charleston?"

She ducked her head and nodded. "Partly, I suppose. Some people can be so unkind. But I do prefer the country life much more than city life." She folded up her stitching and placed it in the cloth bag that she carried it in, looking a bit forlorn.

Touched by the loneliness in her eyes, Adam carefully scooted to the edge of the cot and sat with his elbows on his knees. His hands, clasped together, were mere inches away from hers. "Have you never had any close friends other than the Reeds?"

"No, not really." Hannah shook her head. "I used to spend a lot of time around the barn and watch the men train the new horses, but Dad made me quit after I got older. He said it wasn't proper for a young lady to be spending so much time with so many males."

"Sounds like a wise man."

Hannah looked over at him as if she were checking to see if he were teasing. He held her gaze steadily without flinching.

"I have some friends like Ruthie—the girl who was here the day we found you—but they all live in Charleston.

Occasionally one of them will come and stay a week or two, but most find it boring here." She smiled sweetly; then her gaze darted away.

Adam's heart was touched by her vulnerability. She was so cheerful most of the time that he hadn't stopped to consider she might have problems of her own. He'd been so caught up in his own pain that he hadn't thought about hers. Reaching out, he laid his hand over hers and gave it a gentle squeeze. "It must get lonely sometimes."

"Oh, I don't know." Her brave smile didn't reach her eyes. "It's all I've ever known. I remember being lonely whenever Jamie and Cooper left with their parents to go to Charleston. My father ofttimes traveled with them." She offered him a benign smile. "But I wouldn't trade my life for city life, even if I had hundreds of friends. I love horses and all kinds of animals. I wish I had the freedom to hop in a saddle and ride astride like a man." Her cheeks turned a becoming red. She pulled her hands from his and fiddled with the string of her bag. "There are times I wish I'd been born a boy."

Adam wondered if the subject made her nervous because she was babbling again. "I'm certainly glad you weren't. You're way too pretty to be a boy." Adam couldn't hold back his grin when she blushed again.

"Would you kindly stop saying that?"

"What? That you're pretty? No, I can't, because it's the truth."

Hannah, discomfort written all over her face, jumped to her feet, her chair banging against the wall. "I think I'll be going now and just leave you to yourself."

The cot creaked as Adam slowly stood up. "Hannah, are you mad at me?"

Her head hung down, and she shook it slowly.

"Hannah," he pleaded.

When she didn't look at him, he reached out with two

fingers and tilted her head up. "Hannah, you're beautiful, inside and out, and you deserve to have someone tell you that. You shouldn't be embarrassed about the way God made you. But if it makes you uncomfortable, I'll try to keep my opinion to myself. Though it might be hard to do." He smiled, hoping to reassure her. "Please, let me be your friend."

With a hesitant smile, Hannah glanced up at him. "We *are* friends."

"Good." He grinned and reached his hand out to her. "How about that walk?"

Timidly, Hannah slipped her small hand into his. "All right, but there's only time for a short one. I don't want you to be overdoin' it, and Chesny will grumble all the way home if we don't set out before dark."

They ambled through the house, and he stopped on more than one occasion to inspect something that seemed familiar. Even the floor plan felt recognizable. Had he been in this home before?

He spied an open set of double doors and hurried across the room. He had a need to inhale some fresh air. Stepping into the sunlight that shone in the entryway, he lifted up his face, allowing the fingers of warmth to caress it. Good thing he'd come up when he had or the sun would have sunk below the horizon. "I smell the flowers from the garden."

Hannah stopped beside him. "You shouldn't be standing out in the open. What if those men are keeping watch? They could see you."

He wanted to say he didn't care. But he did. If those men saw him and came here again, they might hurt the women for harboring him. In the condition he was in, he wouldn't be able to fend off one man, let alone three. He heaved a sigh and stepped back into the shadows of the house. At least he was out of that dungeon.

"Fine. Allow me a few minutes to escort a lovely lady

around the house; then I'll head back to my cage." He held out his elbow to her.

She slipped her arm through and walked beside him. "It really isn't a cage, you know. It's meant to protect you."

"I know, but I'd rather be back in that room where I can see the sky out the window and enjoy the light."

She patted his arm. "It's just for a little while. Israel is keeping watch around here and has the field workers also keeping an eye open for the men. Hopefully if they come back, we'll get some warning."

Adam noticed a picture of a ship and crossed the room. He stood, hands behind his back, and gazed at it. "That's a fine schooner there."

Hannah stared at him for a moment. "How do you know it's a schooner?"

He pointed to the sails. "A schooner has two or more masts with sails fore and aft."

"I know what a schooner is, but how is it you know?"

He turned to face her. "I've sailed on one before—with my father."

Hannah clutched his arm. "You remember your father? What's his name?"

Hope poured through his chest as he caught on to her meaning. He'd remembered something of his childhood. He closed his eyes—willing—struggling to grasp hold of the image of a tall man. . .just out of reach. A sharp pain speared his head, and he scowled.

"Stop, Adam. The memories seem to return when you're relaxed, not when you're fighting for them."

She was right, but he was so close. He almost saw his father's image, but his family name remained as elusive as his chances at winning Hannah's heart.

nine

Arms crossed against his chest, one foot resting over the other, Adam relaxed against a huge live oak. The warmth filling him wasn't from finally being out in the bright sunshine, but it came from watching Hannah toss pebbles into the creek that flowed a good distance from the house. Four days had passed, and with no sign of the motley trio that had been searching for him, Hannah had relaxed her stance on keeping him hidden.

Buster splashed in the shallow water, still limping, but getting better each day. He and the dog had made friends, much to his relief.

Hannah cupped her hands into the water and splashed the dog. Adam smiled, surprised at how much he enjoyed her company. In the span of a few short days, they had become close friends. Whenever he was alone in the pit, his thoughts focused on two things: regaining his memory—and Hannah.

His head itched and he reached up, vigorously scratching it. He looked longingly at the water, wondering if there was some way he could bend over enough to wash his hair. Hannah turned and waved at him. Jerking his hand from his head, he waved back, hoping she hadn't seen his uncouth scratching. He lifted his shirt and took a whiff, shamed by his filthy appearance. He had crawled through the dirt, buried himself under hay on the barn floor, and gone days— maybe weeks—without a bath. How could Hannah stand to get within ten feet of him?

She tossed him an I-know-something-you-don't-know smile and walked over to a bag she'd brought with her. Adam watched her slip her hand in, remove something, and turn quickly around, hiding the item behind her back. She walked toward him, her perfect pink lips curled into a bright smile.

"I have a surprise for you." Her teasing expression melted away, and her eyes widened.

"What?" He asked, looking over his shoulder to see if someone was behind him.

"Uh. . .your eyes."

"What about them?" Adam grimaced, looking away, knowing his appearance was appalling. He'd gazed at his reflection in a mirror in the parlor several times the past few days. His injured eye had progressed through a colorful metamorphosis from red to purple and black and was now starting to turn a nauseating greenish-yellow. It gaped open slightly, and he could just barely see out of it. "Looks awful, doesn't it?"

"Uh. . .no. They're so. . .blue."

"Blue?" That was one color he'd missed in the mirror.

"Aye," Hannah said, her face beet red. "And such a beautiful shade of blue."

"So, my eyes are blue. . .and black and green and purple." He chuckled. "They're more colorful than my vivid personality."

Hannah giggled, but her cheeks flamed, and she ducked her head. "It's just that in the dimness of the secret room, I'd never noticed you had such blue eyes. They. . .um. . .always looked darker."

Adam grinned. It pleased him immensely that Hannah was so mesmerized with the color of his eyes. "I guess that's understandable, especially since you've only seen one of them for the most part."

"Your eyes remind me of the Reed men. All of them have beautiful blue eyes."

His smile dimmed. He didn't want Hannah admiring

any other men's features. Kicking a stone, he frowned. He despised the jealousy coursing through him. He'd been reading the Bible Hannah had left downstairs and knew that such a trait wasn't pleasing to God.

"Don't you want to know what your surprise is?"

Adam couldn't imagine what she was holding behind her back. He hoped it was one of those delicious apple pastries she'd brought him the day before.

She walked right up to him and looked him straight in the face. "It's time you got rid of that shaggy stuff on your chin. You're starting to look like Buster." She giggled.

Adam's heart nearly jumped out of his chest when Hannah reached up and ruffled his whiskers. She pulled her hidden hand from behind her back and held up a razor, a horn bowl, and a bar of lathering soap. "So, is it a good surprise?"

Still reeling from her touch, he smiled and nodded. Hannah grabbed his shirtsleeve, dragging him toward the creek. He followed along compliantly, shaking his head and chuckling to himself. *I'm as willing as a calf being led to the slaughtering block.*

"Sit down on that boulder and hold on to the razor. I'll get the soap good and wet."

Adam sat down, rubbing his whiskers. It would feel good to be clean-shaven again. He tried to think if he preferred a beard or not. Nothing came to mind, only the inky darkness that persisted whenever he tried to remember. He sighed in frustration, humbled by being so dependent on a snippet of a woman. Looking down at his calloused hands, he wondered what kind of work had earned him those battle scars. How could a man simply forget everything about himself?

At the sound of Hannah's approach, he looked up. Her hands were covered with a mound of sudsy lather. Her twinkling eyes and mischievous grin set his crazy heart racing again.

"It's difficult to decide where to put this. Your whole body could do with a good scrubbing."

Adam's ears warmed at her comment. He grappled for a response, but none came.

Totally oblivious to how her words embarrassed him, Hannah walked up to him and smiled. Without hesitation, gentle hands smoothed the lather around his cheeks and under his chin. His eyes closed, savoring the moment. He could get used to this treatment quite easily. His eyes popped back open when he felt Hannah tugging on the razor in his hand. When he didn't let go, she looked at him, blue eyes wide open, brows raised in a question. Such beautiful eyes. He loved the way the indigo ring encircled the lighter shade around her pupil.

Adam gripped the razor tighter. "I can shave myself," he said, a bit gruffer than he meant to be. He didn't want Hannah to think he was totally helpless.

"So you can." Relinquishing her soapy hold on the razor, Hannah turned and headed back toward the creek. She stooped down, rinsed her hands, and filled a cup with water. Adam watched her, feeling remorse over his brusqueness.

He flipped the razor open and slid the sharp blade along his jaw and down to his chin, the bristly sound bringing with it a memory he couldn't quite grasp hold of. Hannah returned to his side with the tin cup filled with water, and he dipped in the razor and took another swipe. After several minutes of scraping and dipping, he had a freshly shaved face again. He ambled over to the creek and stiffly stooped down. Careful to not twist his midsection, he dipped the razor in the creek. He dried the razor on his trousers, flipped it shut, and scooped up a handful of water, rinsing the lather residue off his face.

He stood at Hannah's approach. She handed him a dishcloth, and he dried his face, conscious of Hannah's appraising gaze.

"You look much nicer without all that hair on your face." She took the edge of the cloth and reached up, wiping his lip and the bottom of his chin. "Blood. You cut yourself a little bit." Hannah stuck the towel in his face as if to prove her point.

He snatched the towel and dabbed at his lip. He must have gotten a bit too close to his wound.

Hannah stepped back a few steps, putting her hands on her hips and looked up at his head. Her mouth twitched, and she looked as if she were chewing on the inside of her cheek. Golden brows furrowed and then rose as a blaze ignited in her eyes.

Adam sighed, realizing she had just formulated another one of her plans. "What now?" he asked, though not completely sure if he wanted to know the answer.

"Don't think I haven't seen you scratching your head. I would imagine you'd like to wash it?"

"I'd love to, but I don't see how I can since I can't bend over yet."

Taking the razor from him and stuffing it in her pocket, Hannah grabbed his arm and pulled him back toward the boulder. "I have an idea," she said. "Sit yourself down on this rock. No, wait!"

Hannah ran over to her buggy, put the shaving supplies in the back, and yanked off the old quilt that lay on the seat. Adam watched with skepticism as she spread out the blanket on the large, flat boulder, which jutted out over the water.

"Lie down here with your head toward the water."

"You're planning on washing my hair?"

"Yes."

"No, ma'am, you are not." Adam stood his ground, glaring at her. Enough was enough.

"Surely you're not afraid to have your hair washed, are you?" Hannah turned and looked directly at him.

Adam followed the track of her gaze. Jerking his hand down to his side, he realized he was scratching his head again. Against his will, his mouth turned up in an embarrassed grin.

"Hannah, it just doesn't seem proper for you to wash my hair."

"It ain't proper." Chesny stood just inside the tree line, hands on her hips, her lips twisted to the side. "And if'n she do, I'll tan her backside."

Hannah flung her hands out to her sides. "It's just hair. I washed Michael's a time or two when he broke his hand. Adam's not in any shape to be washing it himself." She spun to face him. "And besides, you're miserable. You can hardly keep your hands off your head because it's itchin' so badly."

"It can wait."

"See! It's itching now, is it not?"

Adam yanked his hand back down to his side, chastised that she caught him scratching again. "Oh, all right. But you're not washing it." He cast Chesny a pleading glance.

The older woman nodded. "I don't mind helpin'." She motioned to a nearby boulder. "Sit yo'self down there and let me take off that bandage."

He did as ordered, and Hannah marched off and dropped onto a blanket she'd brought for them to picnic on. He couldn't help grinning at her indignation. He knew she had a good heart and just wanted to help him feel better, but there was an appealing innocence about her that caused her to not make the wisest of choices at times. Perhaps that came into play when she found him in the barn. He imagined most young women would have rushed off out of fear or fainted, but not Hannah. She had boldly tended to him, and he admired her for it. But she needed to learn that some lines couldn't be crossed.

"Hmph. That there wound is lookin' good. Don't see as

why you need a bandage any mo'." Chesny tossed it aside and pushed up her sleeves. "Get yo'self up on that flat rock and lay back."

Again, he obeyed like a boy and lay down on the sun-warmed stone, listening to the trickling water below. Crickets, locusts, frogs, and birds joined together in an entertaining chorus. The warm spring breeze flittered through the emerald canopy of trees overhead, rustling peacefully.

Adam closed his eyes as Chesny scrubbed his head, and he pretended that Hannah was actually tending to him. Everything about Hannah was kind and gentle, unlike Chesny. He'd be lucky if he wasn't bald by the time she was done with his hair. He smiled and refocused on Hannah. He feared he was falling in love with her. But what could a nameless stranger possibly offer a girl like her?

All he knew about himself was that he was used to working hard. The idleness of the past week was making him antsy. He needed to be working—doing something productive. And now he knew for certain that he'd sailed before. Little things kept creeping back into his mind—of climbing the ratlines and staring out at nothing but brilliant blue water as far as the eye could see. And the wind constantly tugging at his clothing and hair, and the fresh scent of the ocean. But the truly important things like who he was and where he'd come from were still a blur in his mind. If only he could remember everything.

"You's done, boy. I had to use that there shavin' soap on yo' hair." Chesny splashed a few more handfuls of water on his head. "You can get up now."

Hannah smiled and stood. "Doesn't that feel so much better?"

He nodded, relishing in feeling halfway clean again. Water ran down the back of his shirt, saturating it and the wrap on his chest. Suddenly there was a loud crack above his head, and he glanced up. Something long and dark fell. It landed right beside him on the boulder.

Hannah squealed. "Snake! Adam, there's a snake on the other side of you."

He didn't take time to think. Bringing his arms protectively across his chest, he flipped onto his left side, and quickly rolled over twice until he dropped to the ground, landing on his knees. With the grace of a grandpa, he scrambled to his feet and grabbed Chesny's hand. He pulled her over to the blanket where Hannah still bounced on her toes, and turned to see where the snake had gone.

He blinked his eyes to make sure he wasn't seeing things. His lips pursed, and he pressed his hand to his aching side. *I don't believe this.*

On the boulder lay not a snake, but a gnarly, grayish-brown tree branch.

A very unlady-like snort erupted from Hannah's mouth, and Adam turned around to see what was wrong. She stood with her lips pulled tightly together, mirth filling her eyes. No longer able to hold back, she burst into laughter, bending over at the waist. Chesny's chuckles rumbled and bounced her shoulders.

Adam realized he had been the brunt of Hannah's childish prank. Was it similar to the kind that Jamie fellow and his brother had played on her? He grabbed hold of his side, still stinging from the sudden exertion. He didn't know whether to be mad or not.

Fighting back another snicker, Hannah looked up at him, semirepentant. "I couldn't help it, Adam. I'm sorry."

"Yes, I can see. You can hardly stop laughing you're so sorry."

Hannah bit her lip until it turned white.

"Go ahead and cackle before you bite a hole in your lip."

Adam leaned over and knocked the dirt off his pants and draped his right arm across his chest.

Hannah sobered immediately. "I truly hope I didn't hurt you."

Chesny walked to the boulder and picked up her scattered supplies, still snickering.

Adam scowled, turned away, and walked back toward the water.

Hannah walked up behind him. She tugged on his sleeve, and he turned to face her.

"Adam, please don't be mad. I was just teasing. I'm truly sorry."

The penitent look on her pretty face and in her watery, blue eyes cut him to the core. He reached out and cupped her velvety cheek with his hand. "I can't stay mad at you, even if I try."

Hannah laid her hands on his arm. "That was a stupid thing I did. I could have caused you more pain. I didn't think about it, I just did it. Being impulsive has always been a problem for me." She ripped her eyes away from his and looked down.

"Like when you found a beat-up stranger in a barn and rescued him?"

Hannah looked up at him, her gaze framed by thick lashes. A small, embarrassed grin flittered on her lips.

His heart did a flip-flop, and he knew in that moment he'd completely lost his heart to the beautiful, young woman.

She reached out and grabbed his hand, then pulled him over to the boulder and picked up the quilt. Handing it to him, she looped her arm through his and propelled him to a grassy spot. Suddenly, she stopped in midstride, and he worked hard not to run into her. She turned to face him. "Oh, here's another present."

He looked down at the comb in her hand and couldn't resist teasing her this time. He bent over at the waist and put his hands on his knees, aiming his head toward her. When she didn't move, he peeked up at her and grinned. "So, you gonna comb my hair for me, or do you think I can do it myself?"

Her nostrils flared, and he thought for a moment she was going to punch him. As she stood there appraising his head, an embarrassed grin tugged at her appealing lips, and she held out the comb. "Touché."

He took the comb but claimed her hand with it. His thumb glided over her soft skin, and she gazed up at him, her mouth slightly open. He swallowed hard, peeking over his shoulder to see where Chesny was, and she stood there staring at him with her arms crossed and brows raised. He cleared his throat and dropped Hannah's hand.

"It's time to eat our lunch," she said, disappointment evident in her voice. Grabbing one edge of the blanket, she pulled it under the shade of a big oak. Then she knelt down and started removing things from the basket she'd brought.

Adam pulled the comb through his hair, hoping to make himself more presentable. She pulled one thing after another from the basket until she'd spread a fabulous array of food before them.

"I hope you like cold chicken."

"Mmm, love it!" Adam laid the comb on the blanket and turned to find Chesny. "Are you joining us?"

She strolled over to him and glanced down. "I reckon it's safe for you two to eat alone. Just don't go lettin' her talk you into takin' no bath." The twinkle in her eye belied the serious tone of her voice. "I be back in a bit with Israel and some fresh clothes; then we'll tend to that task."

He nodded but looked away, uncomfortable with such talk in front of Hannah. Chesny walked to the tree line, turned back, and wagged her finger at him. He knew she was entrusting Hannah to his care, and it meant a lot that she would trust him.

"Look, Adam. I brought cheese, applesauce, biscuits, and blackberry tarts."

He sat and took the chicken thigh she held out to him. "I think I'm in heaven. Great food and beautiful company, what more could a man ask for?"

A name. My own name. The ever-present thought intruded on his happiness.

Hannah's smile faded at his audible sigh. "What's wrong?"

He shrugged. "I just wish I could remember something about myself. It's so frustrating not being able to." He stared out across the water to the trees on the far bank.

Hannah touched his arm. "I'm prayin' for you, Adam. It will all come back one of these days. We just have to be patient. Besides, even if you did remember, you're not ready to travel yet."

Adam rubbed the back of his neck. He could travel if he had to, but where would his memories take him? To a family in another place? To a job? Across the ocean to England?

One thing he did know: regaining his memory would most likely take him away from Hannah. That was something he didn't mind postponing.

ten

Hannah watched the different expressions dancing across Adam's face. What could he be thinking? It must be so hard not knowing who he was.

Realizing she was staring at Adam's striking blue eyes, she looked away. Today was the first time she'd seen him in the full light of day. His eyes were bluer than the clear Carolina sky. . .and there was something—something vaguely familiar about them. The contrast of his long black lashes, which any woman would love to have, framing his azure eyes against his handsome, tanned face was more enticing than a sapphire pendant. Adam's hair, she had discovered, was inky black, not dark brown, as she'd first thought. Hannah ducked her head when she felt her cheeks flame. Her feelings for Adam ran far deeper than was proper for a woman promised in marriage to another man. Was it merely because of the bond created from her saving his life, or because he'd been so dependent on her, or was there more depth to her attraction?

"How do you manage to spend so much time away from your home without anyone missing you?" Adam leaned back on his hands. His long legs stretched out in front of him, hanging off the edge of the blanket.

"My parents have gone to Charleston on business," Hannah said, thankful for the distraction from her errant thoughts. "The Reeds are returning home after a long while away, so I'm seeing that everything here is clean and in order. Michael is busy with the spring planting and doesn't care what I do as long as his meals are seen to."

"That's quite kind of you to take on the task of preparing

this plantation house for its owners. When you marry, your future husband will certainly be blessed having such a lovely and capable woman overseeing his home."

The skin on Hannah's face tightened. She hadn't mentioned to Adam that she was to marry Jamie. Had one of the servants told him, or was he speaking in generic terms?

When he didn't question her, she assumed the latter. The longer she was around Adam, the less appealing marriage to Jamie sounded. What would Jamie expect of her? That was something she'd never considered before. Would he expect her to stick to the house and do all the domestic chores her mother did? Would he want her to travel to Charleston every time he went? Most likely he would. Her days of living mainly on the plantation could be numbered. She plucked a tiny flower and twirled it in her fingers. The truth was she knew very little about Jamie Reed other than that he was handsome and kind.

I wonder what Adam would expect of his wife. Just the thought sent her cheeks flaming again.

"So what can you do besides clean, tend the wounded, and stitch samplers?"

Hannah sat up straighter. "I can cook as well as any of the servants—my mother made sure of that. I'm an expert seamstress and have sewn clothes for our workers' children. I know how to keep books and can play the harpsichord quite well. I don't mind at all tending the plantation, but I can't say I enjoy city life all that much."

"I don't blame you for not wanting to leave. This place is beautiful—and so peaceful." He smiled at her, his eyes warm. "So how about another piece of that delicious chicken you spent all morning cooking?"

She handed him another thigh and took special delight at how he seemed to enjoy her cooking. He picked up the last of the chicken bones from his plate and tossed them in the bushes. "So what would you expect in a wife?"

He shrugged. "The same thing as most men, I suppose. That she be sweet and loving, a good cook, capable of caring for the home and any children we had. I also think it's important that she be a godly woman. I've been reading the Bible and am certain that I believed in God before."

Adam's wife will be a fortunate woman. Hannah leaned back on her hands and stared at the puffy, white clouds overhead and listened to his mellow voice. It lulled her into a relaxed, peaceful state. Her mind drifted, and she wondered what Adam's children would look like. She envisioned cute, tiny versions of him with dark hair and remarkably blue eyes. She watched the children playing in the dirt. Three, no, four of them, two boys and two girls. One little girl with curly blond hair toddled over to Hannah, reaching short, pudgy arms up to her. Hannah smiled and looked down into the child's sweet face. A pair of bright blue eyes stared lovingly back— eyes the same color as Adam's. She sucked in a sharp breath.

Shaken from her daydream, her gaze darted over to him. He licked his fingers and stared at her with a strange expression. Hannah knew he couldn't read her thoughts, but somehow she wondered if he knew she'd been thinking of children—their children. She jumped up and jogged over to the creek. Stooping down, she rinsed the chicken grease off her hands.

I feel as if I've betrayed Jamie. Oh God, how can I be promised to Jamie Reed in marriage and dare think about being Adam's wife and having his children? It's so wrong. Lord, my whole life long I've heard Mama's plans about me marrying Jamie when I'm grown. I never questioned them before, so why am I now? Why did I have to find Adam? Why now, when Jamie will be returning soon? Maybe it was a mistake to take care of Adam as I have.

Instantly, she felt condemnation for her thoughts. If she

hadn't found him, he'd most likely be dead by now. The thought of Adam lying cold and dead on the Reeds' barn floor chilled her. Hannah crossed her forearms and rubbed the goose bumps that had suddenly popped up. In a few short days, Adam had become her best friend.

What should I do, Lord? I can't help the way I feel about him. I like everything about him. I hardly even know Jamie anymore. Please, God, couldn't You work a miracle for me?

"Hannah, are you all right?" Adam had walked up behind her, and she hadn't even realized it. She stood, drying her hands on her skirt, but she didn't turn to him.

What could she say when her emotions were so raw? Adam's fingers came to rest on her shoulders, gently kneading away the tension. "I'm sorry if I said something that upset you."

"It's not you," was all she managed to squeak out.

He stepped beside her, keeping his left arm draped loosely around her shoulders. Why did that feel so right? When she leaned her head against his shoulder, he tightened his grip. She wasn't sure how long they stood there in the quiet setting, serenaded by nature's symphony. The gently moving stream rippled along, birds of all sorts chirped their cheerful songs, while unseen insects hummed their tunes. Hannah appreciated that Adam didn't press her for more information. She just enjoyed the moment. . .because she knew it wouldn't last.

≈

Hannah rocked in one of the four old wooden rockers on the front porch of her family's home.

The barn in the distance stood out as a black silhouette against the evening sky, blazing with the brilliant pinks, oranges, and deep purples of the setting sun. Staring at the beautiful scene, Hannah raised the cup warming her hands and sipped the hot tea. The events of the past few days flashed through her mind as she rubbed the back of her neck with her free hand.

Even though Adam was doing much better, leaving him each evening was getting harder. He had been a model patient. He'd stayed in the cramped little bed without complaining and allowed her to care for him. She smiled as she remembered the conversations they'd had about her family, the checkers games he'd trumped her at, and the times he'd rested while she'd read to him from the Bible or a novel from her father's library. She had faithfully brought him his meals, and he'd rewarded her with his heart-stopping smile.

Hannah looked heavenward and sighed. *Heavenly Father, I'm losing my heart to Adam. He's so easy to talk to. So funny. So patient with my feeble attempts at doctoring. The way he looks at me—as if I'm the most precious thing in all of America—sends shivers through my body. I don't care what his past is or who his family is. Oh, what am I going to do?*

She stared up at the few stars bright enough to be seen in the twilight. Why had she always gone along with her mother's plan for her to marry Jamie? Maybe because she liked him? But if the truth be known, she had always liked Cooper better. Cooper had been her buddy. He'd even written to her many times during the long years he'd been away, but Jamie had only written her a brief note a few times recently.

Hannah sighed and sipped her tea. She'd kept up with Jamie through the letters her mama had received from Heather Reed and with visits when she was home at Reed Springs. Once she had even asked her mother why she had to marry Jamie instead of Cooper. Mama's response was, "He's the oldest, and the oldest marries first." Hannah let the comment resting on the tip of her tongue slide off unsaid. *If the oldest is supposed to get married first, then why do I have to get married before Michael?*

Wasn't there a story in the Bible like that? Who was it?

Joseph? No, it was Jacob. Jacob traveled to the land of his forefathers in search of a woman to marry. He found Rachel and fell in love. But after Jacob had worked for seven years for her hand in marriage, Rachel's father tricked Jacob, and he ended up marrying Rachel's older sister, Leah. Laban had insisted Leah must marry first since she was the oldest.

Rachel must have been heartbroken to have her sister marry her beau. Hannah shook her head. Too bad Jane hadn't married Jamie, then maybe she and Adam would have a chance at a life together.

Rather than dwelling on things beyond her control, Hannah shifted her focus to a happy memory. A smile tilted her lips as she remembered Cooper's youthful gallantry. On the day he left to go to sea as a cabin boy on one of his father's ships, Cooper had handed her a wilted daisy and told her that he would marry her when he grew up if Jamie didn't want to. They had been best friends. Why was it that the people she grew closest to were the ones to leave? First Cooper left—and now he'd never return—and it was only a matter of time until Adam was well enough to move on, too.

The door banged as Chesny walked out onto the porch. Hannah turned her face away and wiped the tears stinging her eyes. Chesny dropped down in the rocker next to hers.

"Tomorrow is the day yo' mama say we oughta take her weddin' dress out of the trunk. The Reeds, they be back soon and yo' mama say they want to have the weddin' right away. With a few adjus'ments, that gown should fit you jes' fine."

Hannah blew out a loud breath.

"Somethin' wrong?" Chesny's chair creaked a steady rhythm as she moved back and forth.

"What if—what if—"

"You ain't havin' second thoughts, are you?"

Hannah huffed out a laugh. "Second and thirds and fourths."

Chesny's chair halted, and she turned toward Hannah. "When'd that start?"

"I don't know. Before Adam came, if that's what you're wondering."

"Humph. I'ma thinkin' that boy is a big part of yo' doubts."

She leaned forward and put her face in her hands. "I don't know what to do. If I don't go through with the wedding, I'll disappoint everyone—Mama, Heather, Jamie—and they're already distraught over Cooper's disappearance."

Chesny patted her back. "Now, now, it ain't all that bad."

"Yes, it is."

"What you need to do is pray about this and talk to the good Lord. He wouldn't have you marry a man that you'd be miser'ble with."

Wiping her face, Hannah sat up. "You're right. I do need to pray more." She'd been so tired each night that she'd almost fallen asleep at supper, and in the mornings, she'd been so anxious to get over to Reed Springs to see how Adam had fared that she hadn't had her normal prayer and Bible reading time in the mornings. That needed to change. She could hardly expect God to speak to her if she wasn't seeking Him each day.

eleven

Hannah pushed open the door to the secret room, her other hand pressed against her stomach, trying to squelch the tingly sensation. She felt as if a passel of lightning bugs danced in her stomach. In her devotional time this morning, she had spent a half hour in prayer, and her desire to see Adam again hadn't lessened one iota, not even after she pleaded with God to remove the desire if it wasn't His will.

When Adam didn't respond, she knocked harder and walked halfway down the stairs. Israel had said Adam hadn't slept well the night before, so perhaps he'd fallen asleep after breakfast. "Adam, are you awake?"

When no answer came and her eyes had adjusted to the dim lighting, she continued down the stairs, her excitement waning, replaced by concern. Had yesterday's outing been too much too soon?

Adam lay scrunched up on the narrow cot, a pile of quilts on the floor. She picked up the covers and laid one over him, then folded the rest and set them on the table. He stirred slightly but didn't awaken. She retrieved his cup from the table, filled it with water from the pitcher, and set it down again.

She had worried about him all night. He had been holding his side ever since she played that snake joke on him. That had been such a foolish act on her part, and she sorely regretted it. She allowed herself a moment to study his sleeping form. His large frame was much too big for the cot. Over six feet tall, he towered over her by a half foot. She remembered the day she'd massaged his neck and shoulders.

His build was lean but muscular, the kind of muscles earned by hard work—and that work must have been done outside, for no man with a desk job would have such sun-kissed skin. She touched her warm cheeks, remembering the pleasantness of his strong arms around her that day the three men came to the house.

Would she feel the same inner delight if Jamie held her? She wished he was still in England—and that thought took her by surprise. When had she started dreading Jamie's return to Reed Springs? She dropped onto one of the chairs and propped her chin up with her hand. Dare she call off the wedding? Her mother and Heather Reed would be so disappointed. And what about Jamie? Did he truly want to marry her?

He was twenty-nine now and surely ready to marry and start a family. She would be hard-pressed to find a man as good and responsible as he. And he was a godly man. But was he the right man?

Adam murmured something unintelligible in his sleep, drawing her gaze to his face. The bruises and cuts were pressed against the bed, leaving his handsome side showing. His chin was fresh-shaven and his hair gleamed like a raven's wing from yesterday's scrubbing. He was a fine-looking man with eyes that reached clear to her soul, but that wasn't what drew her to him. He needed her—and a part of her needed him. She loved his quiet, teasing nature and ached for him to be reunited with his memories.

Reaching down, ever so gently, she brushed a lock of dark hair away from his face. The lantern light danced against his cheek. She stood next to him, admiring his tanned face and his thick, ebony lashes that lay in a half moon against his cheek. Hannah's gaze wandered down to his healed lips.

Adam jerked his head sideways and moaned. "No, not again." He rolled onto his back, his head tossing to one side and then the other. "Won't tell you where it is."

Hannah leaned forward to hear better. He suddenly cast the quilt aside and sat up, and his rock-hard grasp clamped onto her wrist. Stunned, she yelped and attempted to jerk away, but instead of getting free, he pulled her toward him, and she fell across his lap.

With her cheek pressed hard against Adam's stomach, held there by his strong arm, she gazed up at him with fear in her heart for the first time since she'd discovered him in the barn. The disheveled mess of his long, dark hair added to his frightening countenance. The relentless pounding of her heart abruptly stopped at the angry glint in his eyes and snarl on his lips.

❧

Adam held tight to the man who had attacked him. The relentless trio had chased him all the way from Charleston. They meant to take him back—or worse. He had to get away—had some vital information they wanted. He fought the fog threatening to suck him under and forced his eyes open. What he saw drove away all hint of sleepiness. Hannah was crushed against him, held there by his iron-hard grasp. "Hannah?"

"Y–yes, it's m–me."

"My apologies. I didn't realize it was you." He blinked his eyes and squeezed his forehead, trying to understand what was real and what he'd dreamed. "I thought those men were attacking me."

"I can assure you, I have no plans to harm you."

Regret washed over him as he realized he still held her in his tight grip. He gazed down at her and brushed her hair back from her forehead. A smile tugged at his lips. "The thought of you attacking me isn't altogether unpleasant."

For nearly a week, he'd wondered what her hair would feel like. He must have knocked off the linen cap she wore when cleaning. Hannah's wavy mass of hair filled his lap and flowed over the side of the cot. He pick up a strand of pure gold and rubbed it between his fingers. "So soft. So lovely."

He could feel her fervent heartbeat pounding against his thigh.

He loved her. He was certain.

Had he ever been in love before?

I wish I could remember. But surely if I had ever felt like this, I would not have forgotten about it.

Filled with remorse for scaring her half out of her wits, Adam scanned Hannah's lovely face. It no longer held any fear, but rather something else: trust and—affection. This lovely, innocent young woman had stolen his heart in a matter of days. He pulled her into his arms, and with a groan of pent-up longing, he held her close against his chest.

ॐ

Hannah wrapped her arms around Adam's waist, carefully avoiding his cracked ribs. She relished the security of his strong arms around her again. With a mind-opening revelation, she realized what she'd been feeling for this man whom she knew nothing of a few days ago, must be love. She'd read the Song of Solomon and talked to her friends about falling in love, but never dreamed it could happen to her.

When Adam released her slightly, Hannah stared up at him, biting her lip to stop its trembling. Though he no longer held her imprisoned within his powerful grasp, the expression on his handsome face held her captive. Hannah couldn't hold back the contented sigh that slipped out. The crooked grin on Adam's lips made her smile.

"Hannah, my angel, do you know what I'm thinking?"

Slowly, she shook her head, mesmerized by his compelling gaze.

"I'm thinking I want to kiss you." He brushed her cheek with the back of his fingers. "Would that be all right with you?"

Surely, one kiss couldn't hurt anything, could it? After a moment's hesitation, she nodded. Hannah licked her lips in anticipation of her first kiss. Her throat thickened, and she held her breath when Adam leaned toward her. She stretched her arms around his neck and ran her fingers through the dark hair hanging past his collar as he placed an achingly sweet kiss on her lips. His warm lips lingered. When she responded with enthusiasm the kiss turned a corner from sweet to intense.

Adam groaned, whether in pain or emotion, she didn't know. Suddenly, he pulled away and set her roughly on the ground. Hannah blinked and stared up at him. Confusing thoughts swarmed her mind. *What did I do wrong?*

"I'm sorry." He leaned back against the wall and forked his hair back from his face.

"Why?" she whispered, completely bewildered.

"Hannah, you shouldn't be here alone with me like this."

"I don't understand. You wouldn't hurt me, would you?"

"No. Not in the sense you mean." Adam smacked his fist against the cot. "I don't trust the way I'm feeling right now, and besides, you don't know a thing about me. I may be a highwayman, an escaped convict—or something worse."

"No." Hannah shook her head. "There's a gentleness in you, and I'm sure you'd never do anything against the law or anything to hurt me."

"No matter—the sooner I find out who I really am and get out of here, the better it will be for you."

Hannah pushed to her feet and nailed him with an angry look as she grappled for a response. She blinked, trying desperately to hold back her tears. *How could he think of leaving when he has just turned my world upside down with one kiss?*

As she opened her mouth to snap at him, she heard Chesny's call. Ducking her head to hide the tears streaming down her cheeks, she turned and fled. For once, she had to get away from this perplexing man.

❧

Hannah pounded the bread dough with all her might. *What did I do wrong? Was my kiss so bad?* She punched and rolled and beat the dough some more.

"That bread'll be hard as a stone if'n you don't stop beatin' it." Chesny stared at her with her hands on her hips.

Could Adam have disliked my kiss so much that it repulsed him? His kiss was wonderful—she sighed and slapped the dough again—*until he dumped me on the floor. I just don't understand.*

"What's got into you, child?"

"Did you love Peter when you two got married?"

Chesny's eyes widened. "Well, 'course I did, or I wouldn't have married him. Why're you askin' me such a thing?"

"I guess I've been thinking of marrying Jamie. I don't even know him anymore. He's been working in Charleston for so many years and rarely returns to Reed Springs."

"That Jamie, he's a good boy and he'll take good care of you."

Not wanting to get flour in her hair, Hannah used her forearm to push some wayward tendrils of hair from her face. "How long did you know Peter before you knew you loved him?"

"Don't rightly know. We didn't see each other often, what with him workin' the fields and me in the house." Chesny's lips lifted in a soft smile. She reached up and patted her hair as if preparing to see her husband, who'd been dead four years.

"It all started with a look. That Pete, he would stare at me likes I was somethin' special. I grew to look fo'ward to seein' him of a evening. I grew to respect Peter, 'cause he was a hard worker and took good care of his mammy. Eventually that respect bloomed into affection and affection grew into love. One day I realized I was in love with that tall buck, and we jumped the broom."

Hannah watched Chesny staring off as if seeing her beloved again. She and Peter were married ten years before he got hurt in an accident and died the next day. She could still remember crying because her nanny was so sad for so long—but at least she got to marry the man she loved.

"But what if I never learn to love Jamie? Maybe Jamie won't even like me. He probably prefers city women now to the backward daughter of a planter."

"What's bringin' on all these strange ideas, girl?" Chesny picked up a paring knife and began to cut up some strawberries. "Don't you fret now. Jamie, he always was a handsome boy, and he come from a good family. Everythin'll work out fine, you'll see."

Hannah tore the dough in half and patted one part into a loaf and placed it in the pan.

"You had a fondness for that boy when you was young. You'll rekindle that attraction once you spend time with him again."

"I had a fondness for *both* Jamie and Cooper as boys. I felt like I'd lost two brothers when they rode out of my life." Hannah stared at Chesny. "That's how I think of Jamie, as another brother. Marrying him would be like marrying Michael." Hannah shivered at the thought.

Chesny put her hands on her waist, scrunched her eyebrows together, and pursed her lips. "Miz Hannah, let's have none of that silly talk. Mastah Jamie is not yo' brother. He will be yo' husband. Yo' mama has her heart set on that."

"But she said the oldest should marry first, and she hasn't found anyone for Michael, and he's older than me. Besides, this is America. Arranged marriages aren't so common here." She tried to calm her steadily rising volume. "What if I don't want to marry Jamie?"

"And who else would you be wantin' to marry?" Chesny straightened her spine and narrowed her eyelids. "Certainly not that Adam. Or meb'be you'd prefer yo' parents marry you off to one of them ol' widow men from town? One with a whole passel of child'en already?"

Hannah felt the color drain from her face. She knew the truth. There *were* plenty of men in the town who would be thrilled to marry a young woman from a prominent family like hers.

"I heard yo' daddy tell yo' mama that he done had more than a few inquiries from interested gentlemen." Chesny's expression softened. "You don't like livin' in town all the time, and if'n you marry Jamie, you might not have to, bein's as he's so understandin' and all."

Hannah felt sure she'd die if she had to spend the rest of her life in town—never able to walk in the gardens or ride across the open fields in her buggy, unable to visit her favorite thinking spot down by the creek. She had to tell Chesny what was on her heart. "I. . .I'm just not sure that the good Lord wants me to marry Jamie Reed."

"Well then, you'd better pray hard that He be speakin' to yo' mama and yo' daddy and tell them the same thing. The Bible says that child'en are to honor and obey their parents."

"Oh, it's hopeless! They'll never understand," Hannah cried. She turned and ran out the door. Its slam echoed behind her as she raced toward the barn and the comfort of the animals.

twelve

Adam paced the length of the small *dungeon* and back. Pausing for a moment, he peeked up the stairway, but there was no sign of Hannah. She must have fled back to the safety of her home, or else she was working in some obscure region of the Reed house, because she hadn't been back to see him all day.

His stomach rumbled, once again notifying him that he had missed lunch. How could he eat when he'd done such a foolish thing? "I never should have kissed Hannah. I barely know her." The memory of her warm kisses and the feelings they stirred within him, irritated him. He turned and kicked one of the table legs, sending his mug of water tumbling to the dirt floor.

If he truly loved her as he believed he did, the best thing he could do was to stay away from her. Adam tiptoed up the stairs and peeked into the dining room. Seeing no sign of anyone and sick of being cooped up, he left the confines of the secret room and headed for the nearest door. The woods and water called to him. As deeply as his bound-up chest would allow, he breathed in the fresh spring air. Once in the shelter of the trees, he paced back and forth, trying to sort out his emotions.

Why can't I remember who I am? How can I have such strong feelings for a woman I've just met? Why did I have to hurt her like that? He felt like he'd been gut shot at the hurt and confusion in Hannah's blue eyes, as she sat on the floor where he'd dropped her after their wonderful kiss.

He knew she was attracted to him. He could tell by the

way she looked at him and how she responded to his kiss. "Show me what to do, Lord. Don't let there be anything in my past that could hurt Hannah."

Adam stopped pacing and looked up through the trees to the bright blue sky. It suddenly dawned on him that he'd been praying. It had been such a natural thing to do. Hour after hour of Bible reading had solidified any doubts that he believed in God. Talking to God seemed so right that he knew he was a believer. A warm peace filled his whole being.

Behind Adam, a twig snapped. The nearby bushes rustled with movement, and he froze. He had the unnerving feeling he was being watched.

Then Hannah stepped out from behind a huge tree.

"Hannah." He offered a smile, but the apology stuck in his throat.

She returned his smile with a feeble one and kept her head down. She wrung her hands together.

He walked to her and took hold of her hands, but she didn't look up. He'd really hurt her by his actions. He felt lower than a worm. "I. . .uh. . .feel bad that I kissed you this morning."

She sighed and batted her lashes as if she had dust in them.

When she didn't look up, he cradled her cheeks and lifted her face. The unshed tears shining in her eyes rent his heart. "I apologize."

"Shh," came her soft response. "It's not as if you didn't ask permission."

"Tell me what's wrong."

She shrugged and lowered her gaze.

Tiny chills raced up Adam's spine. Hannah's head nearly rested against his chest. He fought the urge to wrap her in his embrace. Wisps of her hair tickled his chin. Adam couldn't breathe, but he was sure the snug binding around his chest was not the reason.

Hannah finally looked up. Their faces were inches apart, and Adam could feel her warm breath on his face. She blushed and started to back away, but he reached behind her with one arm and pulled her close again. "Did anyone ever tell you that you're an angel?"

A melancholy smile danced on Hannah's lips. "Just you."

"Guess I did, didn't I?"

"Yes."

Adam ran the back of his fingers down her cheek. "Well, it's true."

"I doubt if my mother would agree. I've caused her more than her share of worries over the years, and I'm sure Michael thinks I'm more devil than angel."

"You've earned the title by rescuing me."

Adam continued to hold her gaze. He wished more than anything that he could spend the rest of his life right here. Long tendrils of Hannah's hair curled playfully around her face. He wanted to kiss her again. The audible grumble in his stomach brought just the diversion he needed.

Hannah's lips twitched. "You wouldn't be hungry, perchance?"

He patted his stomach. "My angel deserted me at lunchtime, and I didn't have much of an appetite."

Hannah pushed out of his embrace. "I'm sorry."

"You have nothing to be sorry about. I chased you away. I never should have kissed you like I did."

Her head hung down again. "It wasn't your kiss that caused me not to come back," she whispered softly.

"Then what did?"

When she didn't respond, Adam reached out and touched her shoulder. "What is it, Hannah? What upset you?"

"Umm. . .I don't know." She shrugged.

Adam tightened his grip on her shoulders. "Come on, tell me what's the matter."

Her brows dipped down, and her nostrils flared. "Fine, then. After you kissed me, you threw me on the floor like I was poison. You couldn't get away fast enough." She looked up, tears flooding her eyes and running down her cheeks. "What did I do wrong?"

He caressed her shoulders. "Oh, angel. *You* didn't do anything. It was me."

"You?" Her innocence and trust wrenched his insides worse than the beating had. She had no idea what she did to him.

"Hannah, I didn't want our kiss to end. It was something so special," he said, caressing her cheeks. "I guess it scared me when I realized that I've come to care so deeply for you so fast. I don't want to hurt you, and I sure didn't mean to upset you. Please, forgive me."

"Let's not talk about it anymore." Hannah shook her head, and they shared a smile. "I feel the same way."

"All right, we won't mention it again then." He pulled her to him and wrapped his arms around her, resting his chin against her hair as Hannah's arms encircled his waist.

All too soon, the grumbling in his stomach became too much to ignore. Hannah started giggling against his chest, and Adam found himself laughing, too.

"If the stomach is the way to a man's heart, I guess I had better get busy and feed you."

&

Hannah wiped the porcelain statue with the dust cloth, while her thoughts wandered back to a Bible verse she had read just that morning: *"Trust in the Lord with all thine heart; and lean not unto thine own understanding. In all thy ways acknowledge him, and he shall direct thy paths."*

I'm trying not to lean on my own understanding, but it's so hard, Lord. I don't understand what's happening between Adam and me. Why did You bring him into my life? Why did I have to fall in love with him? What do I do about Jamie? I don't want to hurt or embarrass him, but how can I marry him when I care so much for Adam? Show me a way out of marrying Jamie, if it's possible. Please.

Hannah sighed and set the statue down. She knew in her heart God was directing her to tell Adam about Jamie, but so far she hadn't been able to bring herself to do so. She didn't want to lose him when she had just found him.

"You sure ain't very good comp'ny today." Chesny fluffed up a pillow on Lucas and Heather Reed's bed, then flipped the quilt over it.

"I'm sorry. Just a lot of things on my mind, I suppose." Hannah swiped the thin layer of dust off a side table with her rag.

"Meb'be it's time you wrote yo' mama a letter and told her what all you been a thinkin'."

Hannah's gaze darted to Chesny. "I can't do that. She'd never understand."

"Meb'be she understand mo' than you give her credit fo'." Chesny shrugged. "I'ma goin' back down to the kitchen and he'p Leta with supper."

Hannah knew what would happen if she wrote to her mother. Caroline Madison would be on the first ship inland. Perhaps she would have better success writing to her father. He always was a softie where his daughter was concerned. And what about the Reeds? Could she actually break off the wedding, which would most likely cause them distress, when they were still searching for Cooper and hadn't accepted that he was probably dead?

She pressed her hand to her heart, hoping that wasn't the case. Perhaps Cooper had left college early for some reason and set sail for home. Perhaps the ship had sunk in a storm, but Coop had survived and was stranded on a tropical island like Robinson Crusoe. Or perhaps his ship's captain had changed their course and set sail for a distant land. There could be a myriad of reasons why Coop had gone missing, but she refused to believe that the fun-loving youth she had been so close to was dead.

She glanced around the room to see what else needed attending. A desk sat in the corner, ready for its owner to return. She knew there was paper in the drawer, but could she actually write a letter? What could she say? "Dear Father, I can't marry Jamie because I've fallen in love with a man who doesn't know his name."

She heaved a sigh. It sounded so absurd. And though she would be happy—relieved—to have the truth come to light, everyone she knew would be disappointed. Jamie would be hurt. But wouldn't he be hurt even more in the long run if she married him, knowing she could never love him as he deserved to be loved?

A board in the floor creaked, and she spun around, one hand splayed across her chest. Her eyes widened and her mouth dropped open but nothing came out. Adam stood there with a stupid grin on his face. Had he heard the words she'd voiced out loud? She heaved her arm back and threw the dust cloth at him. It bounced benignly off his chest, and he caught it. "Y–you shouldn't sneak up on people like that."

His grin grew bigger. "I wasn't sneaking, I was looking for you."

She pivoted away and moved some things around on the desk. He crossed the room, and his hands lightly grasped her shoulders, then he turned her to face him. Crossing her arms over her chest, she ducked her head and refused to look at him. What must he be thinking?

"Look at me, Hannah."

"No."

"Did you mean what you said or was it just a slip of the tongue?"

When she didn't respond, Adam reached out with two

fingers and lifted her chin. Though her head came up, she refused to raise her eyes to his.

"Hannah, don't be embarrassed. It warmed my heart to hear those words fall from your lovely mouth."

After a long moment, she dared to peek up at him through her lashes. He truly sounded as delighted as his smile indicated.

"Listen to me. I *love* you." Adam cupped her cheeks with his hand, and she couldn't resist closing her eyes and leaning in to his caress. "There's no use fighting it. I've tried but I can't deny the truth. I know I've only known you a week, but I love you with all my heart. Dare I hope what I heard you say was the truth? Do you—can you—feel the same for me?" The hope in his beautiful blue eyes dissolved her resolve to be upset with him.

"You know I do."

Adam's whole face brightened with a huge grin. Hannah smiled in response to his boyish enthusiasm. He pulled her into his embrace, and she leaned her head up as his lips found hers. All too soon, he pulled away, but this time he held on to her, cuddling her against his chest.

"I never knew it could feel so good to love someone," Adam whispered against her lips. His breath carried the scent of the coffee he'd recently drunk.

Thoughts of betrayal to Jamie and his displeasure with her behavior invaded her happiness. With a heavy sigh, she leaned her cheek against Adam's warm chest, and his heart raced beneath her ear. Adam's hand left her waist, and tingles coursed down her spine as he slowly caressed her back.

After a moment of enjoying their closeness, she pulled herself free of his embrace, feeling the need to put some distance between her and Adam.

"Is something wrong?"

She hated the concern that stole the happiness from his

gaze. "There's something we need to talk about."

"Fine, but first I want to hear you say it again."

"Say what?" she asked, knowing good and well what he wanted to hear.

"Hannah, please, I need to hear the words. . .to know you meant it."

She tilted her head back, looked deeply into his eyes, and flashed him a dazzling smile. "I love you, Adam. . .whoever you really are."

"What if I'm some horrible person?" he asked hesitantly, then looked away.

Hannah cupped his cheeks with her hands and forced his gaze back. "It matters not. It's you I love and not who or what you are, though I can't believe there's anything all that dreadful in your past."

Adam's grip tightened on her waist. "I love you also, Hannah. So much, it hurts."

"Me, too, but we must talk about some other things—important things," she said, with a measure of dread.

"All right then. Come on." He took her hand. "Let's go outside and walk for a while."

"Do you think it's safe?"

Adam shrugged. "I don't know, but I can't stand being cooped up inside any longer. We'll stick close to the trees and use them for cover." Hand in hand, they followed the creek as it wound its way across the heart of Reed Springs.

"I've been remembering some things."

Hannah looked up and caught Adam's gaze. "I'm pretty sure now that the brown-haired woman I keep seeing is my mother. I see her in a kitchen, wearing an apron, and she has flour all over her hands. The dream is so real, I can even smell her fresh bread. The man. . .I don't know. He could be my father, but he seems younger."

"Perhaps, he's your brother or a friend."

"It's possible. But there's more. . .something about some information."

"What kind of information?"

He shook his head. "I'm not sure, but I think I was supposed to deliver something to someone important—I just wish I could remember." He squeezed the bridge of his nose with his fingertips.

Hannah scooted closer, hooking her arm through his. "It's coming, Adam. Just give it some more time. You're beginning to remember."

"I'm just impatient. I know that there can't be anything serious between us until I figure out who I am."

"It's serious already, don't you think?"

He cocked his head and smiled, drawing his fingertips down her cheek. "Yes, my angel, but I mean I can't ask your father for your hand in marriage until I know."

Hannah's heart jolted, and she placed her hand on his chest. "You want to marry me? B–but what if you never remember?"

"One thing I do know is that I have a faith in God. I've caught myself praying on several occasions over the past few days, and that feels so right. I know I believe in the good Lord. I'm certain He brought us together, and I trust He will help me to remember my past so we can be together always."

"I'm so glad to hear you say that. I believe the same." Hannah's heart raced. She knew the time had come to share her secret, but she dreaded it fiercely. "My situation may be even more difficult for Him to work out than yours."

Hannah turned and walked a short distance away, summoning her courage. She finally turned back toward him. "You believe me when I say that I love you, don't you?"

"Yes, I do," he responded with a nod as he gazed deeply into her eyes. "But what's wrong?"

"Oh Adam," she whispered, as tears coursed down her cheek.

He walked to her, framed her face with his hands, and wiped her tears with his thumbs. "Shh. . . It'll be all right. Just tell me what is wrong, and we'll sort it all out."

"I don't see how." She twisted her hands. "Oh, I should have told you sooner. I. . .I'm promised in m–marriage to a man I hardly know anymore."

thirteen

As if weighted down with cannonballs, Adam's hands fell to his sides. He squeezed his eyes closed while his mind tried to absorb what Hannah had said. He moved away from her and leaned back against the tree, his hand covering his aching heart. Promised in marriage? How could she return his kisses and profess her love to him when she was pledged to another man?

It couldn't be true. This must be some kind of horrid prank.

Jolted back to the present, he realized Hannah had been calling his name. He looked up just in time to see her squeeze past him. Adam called to her and reached out, but grabbed only a handful of air. "Hannah. . .wait."

She ran toward the house. He pushed away from the tree he'd been leaning on and kicked into a run. Each quick step he took jarred his side, but he ignored the pain. In a matter of seconds, his long legs enabled him to catch up with her. He grabbed hold of her arm and jerked her to a stop.

"Stop—please." Holding his side with his free hand, he desperately fought to catch his breath. He leaned against the stair railing, sucking in sharp gasps, and he pulled Hannah into his arms. Her tears bled through his clean shirt and into his chest bindings. She put her arms around his waist and continued to sob.

"Shh. . . I told you—everything will work out." He held her securely in his embrace.

"I don't see how it can."

"I don't either, but I do know God wouldn't have brought

us together like this if He didn't have a special plan for us."
Adam brushed his hand down Hannah's back. "People don't
fall in love when they first meet. It isn't normal. Trust me,
angel. It will all work out."

Adam didn't know how long they stood there together,
his arms wrapped securely around her, offering comfort, and
he receiving comfort from her. He dashed a prayer to God,
asking Him to work a miracle.

Hannah finally relaxed. "I'm so glad you know. I've been so
afraid to tell you. At first it didn't matter, but each day as my
love grew, I became more hesitant to mention it to you."

"Don't ever be afraid to tell me anything." Adam leaned his
chin against Hannah's head. "It's better to know what you're
up against—it's easier to fight it if you know." That sounded
like good advice—if only he could believe it. How could
he fight an arranged marriage when he didn't know a thing
about himself? He swallowed the lump in his throat. "Tell
me about this man you're promised to."

Hannah pressed her cheek against his chest as if she
needed a greater sense of security to broach the subject, and
Adam tightened his grip on her, glad none of the servants
were nearby. "You know how I told you that my family's
closest friends live here. My father and Lucas Reed are old
friends, as is my mother and Heather Reed. When I was
born, Jamie showed a lot of interest in me. He carried me
around and made toys for me, and our parents all thought
it darling. Well, our mothers put their heads together and
decided to arrange a marriage. It's Jamie, the eldest of the
Reed sons, whom I'm promised to."

Jamie. Now he understood the significance of that name.
"Why don't they live here?"

Hannah ducked her head. "It's a sad thing—Cooper,
Jamie's younger brother, has disappeared from the college
he attended in England. The Reeds sailed to England to see

if they could track him down or find some clue as to what happened to him."

Adam's mind struggled to absorb all she'd said. He had to figure out a way to combat this unknown competitor. "So are they coming back here? Or are you just supposed to leave the home you love so much and live in the city you dislike? Or will he marry you and then just leave again?"

Hannah closed her eyes, as if his words hurt her. He pursed his lips, frustrated with the bitterness he'd allowed to seep into his voice.

"Didn't I tell you they were returning soon? That's why I'm getting the house ready. Everyone will return in the next few weeks to prepare for the. . .the wedding." She half-choked on the last words.

"So, you plan to marry a rich man?" Adam relaxed his hold on Hannah, but didn't release her. He didn't bother to hide his disappointment. How could he compete with a wealthy businessman and landowner? He had nothing to offer her—except himself.

"No, Adam." Hannah reached up and cupped his cheek with her hand. "You're the only man I want to marry."

Her sincerity touched him deep within, and his anger focused on the people who would force her to marry a man she didn't love. He reached out and touched a lock of hair that had escaped her cap. He rubbed the soft, golden strands between his fingertips. "Are you sure? You'd marry me not knowing anything about me?" A little laugh escaped his lips at the ridiculousness of his question, and he looked away. He didn't dare hope she'd answer yes. Women needed security, a place to establish roots.

She grabbed his upper arms and shook him, drawing his gaze back. "I know all I have to. You're a kind, gentle man who loves God, and you love me. What else do I need to know?"

"I can't even give you a last name," he whispered, his voice husky and his throat tight.

"You will, you'll see."

He gently set her back from him. He couldn't do it. It wasn't fair to her. "No, Hannah, I can't marry you until I know for sure. If I've done something illegal, I may have to go to jail, and I won't put you or your family through that kind of embarrassment."

"But I just said it doesn't matter to me." Her shoulders drooped, and her eyes held the confusion he knew her heart felt.

Adam wanted to pull her back into his arms, then run off and find a minister who could marry them right away. Instead, he crossed his arms over his chest. "But it does matter to me. I can't ask you to take my name until I know what it is. And there's the matter of your intended, who needs to be dealt with."

"How can you be so unreasonable? If you truly loved me, it wouldn't matter about your name." Hannah turned and stomped off. Then she stopped and spun back toward him, tears coursing down her cheeks. "How can you stand there and say you love me—want to marry me—but then say we can't be together. I don't understand. So you're going to reject me...again?"

He swallowed hard, hating that there was another valid reason for pushing her away, but he had to voice it. "What if. . ." He caught her wounded gaze and sent what he hoped was an apologetic look. "What if I'm already married?"

Her chin wobbled, and tears glimmered in her sad eyes. She turned and ambled away, looking utterly defeated.

He felt as if someone had stabbed him in the heart, but he didn't know what else to say, so he kept quiet and let her go. If he gave her time to collect her thoughts, maybe she'd come around and see that he was right. There were too many unsettled issues standing between them for them to consider a future together at this time. He walked out onto the piazza and leaned on the railing. The last twenty-four hours, his first active day since he'd acquired his injuries, had been exhausting—both emotionally and physically. Maybe if he gave Hannah some time alone, she wouldn't be so upset. He flicked an ant off the rail and heaved a heavy sigh.

Perhaps taking a walk in the gardens would help.

Probably not, but what else did he have to do?

He wandered through the gardens, enjoying the flowers' sweet scents and the feel of the sun on his face. He walked the paths, wondering the whole time if he was making a mistake where Hannah was concerned. But how could a gentleman—a man of honor—do any less?

He had to know his past before he could have a future with Hannah.

A horse's whinny pulled him out of the garden and toward the barn. He needed something physical to do, no matter how small. Perhaps he could groom a horse or two. As he approached the barn, he noticed Israel walking toward him leading a handsome dun. The animal limped slightly, and its front legs were scraped and bloody. What had happened to the poor creature?

Like a lightning flash, a blaze of recognition zigzagged across Adam's mind. A loud gasp escaped his lips. He could see the horse rolling toward him as clearly as if it were the day of the accident. That horse was the one he stole in Charleston so he could make his getaway. The very same horse that had fallen and rolled over him.

"Israel, where did you find that animal?"

"Down in the southernmost field. I done saw 'im two days ago, but he wouldn't let me get near till now."

Adam patted the horse's neck and walked to his other side, not surprised to see a slice in the animal's hide where the lead ball had grazed him. The roll the horse took had coated the injury with a layer of mud, which probably helped it to heal. "This is the horse I was riding the day I was injured." He moved to the front of the horse and stooped. "See here." He pointed to the animal's knees. "He stumbled and fell to his knees, and I flew over his head. Then the horse turned a flip, going down the hill, and rolled over me."

Israel shook his head. "The good Lord was'a watchin' over you, I'ma thinkin'."

Adam nodded his head. "I do believe you are right. Let's take this guy into the barn. He deserves a good meal and some tender loving care."

Israel put the horse in a stall, unsaddled him, and then gave him some fresh hay. While the horse ate, Adam combed its mane and tail, then brushed down the dun's hide. Tomorrow, he would take the horse to the creek and wash him off. The animal probably saved his life as much as Hannah had.

Somehow, he'd have to get the horse back to Charleston and to his owner. The saddle had B. R. engraved in the pommel. Perhaps the tavern owner would know whom it belonged to. Adam swallowed hard. A man could spend years imprisoned for horse stealing. He doubted the fervent need to get away from the men who sought to capture him would be considered much of an argument in the eyes of a judge. Just one more reason he shouldn't put too much hope into a future with Hannah.

≈

Hannah slumped in the buggy seat, exhausted from her physical labors and the mental and emotional turmoil of the day.

"Looks like some folks is at yo' place." Chesny held her hand over her brow to block the setting sun and sat up straight, looking past Simeon.

Hannah, too, looked toward her home. As the fiery orange orb of the sun ducked behind the large Madison barn, her gaze came to rest on a group of people moving in the shadows. She recognized her father's tall, stout form. "They're home! Hurry, Simeon!"

A few minutes later, the buggy pulled to a quick stop in the yard. Hannah didn't wait for help, but instead jumped out into the arms of her father. "How's my Hannah girl?" Richard Madison twirled her around in a circle as he'd done every time he returned home from a journey.

"I'm fine, Papa. How was Charleston? Did you bring me anything? Where's Mama?"

"Whoa now, slow down a bit. You sound just like you did when you were a girl." Her father pushed her back away from him, and his wide grin narrowed into a scrutinizing stare. "You look different. Did something happen while I was gone?"

"W—what do you mean?" Could it be true people could tell someone was in love just by the way they looked? Hannah steeled her features into what she hoped was a natural expression.

"I don't know." He shook his head and smiled. "I suppose my little girl's just growing up." Her father turned and said something to one of the workers as Michael approached.

"You've sure been keeping scarce lately, sis. I'd think you'd be over at Reed Springs enough when you marry that you wouldn't need to spend every day there now."

"Feeling a little neglected?" Hannah threw her arms around her brother's trim waist and looked up into his handsome, tanned face.

"Perhaps just a bit. You've been gone so much I was halfway surprised you didn't sleep over there, too." Michael grinned and tweaked the end of her nose.

She loved her brother and cherished his rare hugs, but her thoughts were on another man—a man whose arms she wished she could stay in the rest of her life.

fourteen

The next morning the whole Madison family was once again seated around the old wooden table in the dining room, enjoying a special breakfast of beef steaks, omelets, biscuits and gravy, and spiced apples. Hannah smiled to herself as she watched her father swirl his coffee around in his cup. It was a habit that she always enjoyed watching. She often teased him about swirling his coffee because he drank it black—it wasn't as if he was trying to mix it up.

Hannah squirmed as she realized her father was staring back at her, his expression unreadable. *He knows something he's not telling me. Could he possibly have found out about Adam?* Hannah's face tightened under his intense scrutiny, and she felt sure the color must have drained from her face.

"What in the world is wrong with you, sis?"

"What do you mean?" Hannah turned toward Michael.

"You look like you're about to take on the world. What's goin' on in that pretty little head of yours?" Michael teased.

"Nothing, I. . .uh. . .was thinking about some things, that's all."

"Well, you're about to have a few more things to think on, isn't that right, Caroline?" Her father smiled and looked over to her mother.

"Of course you are, dear." Her mother's countenance beamed as she reached into her pocket and pulled out a folded piece of paper. She waved the beige paper in Hannah's direction.

She scooted back in her chair and sat up straighter. "What is it?" she asked, feeling more than a little trepidation. The tablecloth, wadded into a hard ball in her fist, matched the

114

tight lump suddenly forming in her throat.

"Why, it's a letter from my best friend, Heather Reed. She says they planned to leave England on April fifth to come back home. That was three weeks ago. They should be arriving any day now, and we'll be having a wedding." Her mother smiled as if all her dreams were coming true—and weren't they? Her dreams, not Hannah's.

Stomach churning at the news, Hannah fought for an acceptable response. She thought she and Adam would have plenty of time for him to remember who he was before her parents and the Reeds returned, but now it seemed that Jamie could show up at her doorstep any day and expect her to marry him. "Um. . .and what news has there been of Cooper? Did they find him?"

Her mother's smile dimmed. "Sadly, no. There has been no sign of him since the day he went cavorting with his two friends. None of them have been heard from since."

"But they don't want to postpone the wedding any longer," her papa said. "With Cooper's disappearance, it's all the more important that Jamie marry and father an heir."

Hannah stared at her plate, no longer hungry. Her papa made her sound like some kind of broodmare.

She couldn't help feeling a little sorry for Jamie. He was being herded to the altar every bit as much as she. Was he also having second thoughts?

An hour later, Hannah climbed out of the buggy and hurried to the secret room. She stepped through the doorway and called down the stairs, "Adam, where are you?"

"He ain't down there," Maisy called from the dining room. "He be out at the barn."

Hannah nodded her thanks and hurried back outside, passing Chesny. The woman just shook her head and went on inside. The creaking barn door grabbed Hannah's attention, and she stopped in her tracks. Adam stepped out of the building, and his haggard expression startled her. Something had happened. She raced to his side and put her hand on his arm. "Adam, are you sick?"

"Something like that," he sighed heavily, his voice filled with anguish. The pained expression on his face took her breath away. Dark shadows rested beneath his eyes. The teasing spark of love and playfulness normally centered in his blue gaze had faded to something that chilled Hannah all the way to her toes.

She threw her arms around his waist and held him tightly, feeling the thudding of his heart against her cheek. He barely put his limp arms around her, and he did not hug her back. As she pulled away and looked up at him, the anguished look in his face tore at her heart like a dull knife.

"What is it, Adam? Didn't you sleep? You look like you've been up all night."

"No. I didn't sleep at all." He ran his hand through his already disheveled hair.

"Why? Are you sick, then?"

Adam placed his hands on her upper arms and tightened his grip. "No. . .uh, yeah, I guess I am. Sick at heart. Hannah, look at me."

She couldn't for the life of her figure out what could have caused the tortured pain in her beloved's eyes. He took a deep breath and his words rushed out. "I've finally remembered my name—and everything else."

Hannah reached out, placing her hand on Adam's cheek. "Glory be, that's wonderful news!" She exhaled a tiny giggle. "I guess I shouldn't call you Adam anymore. So, go on with you. . .what's your real name?"

"It's—Reed."

"Reed?" The words left her mouth, whispered on waves of disbelief. She templed her fingers over her mouth.

"Yes, Hannah, and my mother is Heather Reed."

"I don't understand." She studied him, and the longer she did, the more she knew the truth. He had all the characteristics of the Reed men, save one. He had the black hair, the amazing blue eyes, but the dimples were missing. "You're not Jamie. And Cooper is dead. So, who are you?"

"Cooper isn't dead." His voice, though quiet, held an ominous tone.

Hannah's heart leaped to learn that her old friend might still be alive. "If he isn't dead, then where is he? His family has looked everywhere for him."

"Everywhere but at home." He squeezed his eyes shut for a moment and took a deep, shuddering breath. When he reopened them, Hannah felt icy shivers of apprehension racing down her spine.

"I'm not Jamie—I'm Cooper."

❧

"What?" Hannah felt her world spinning. She stared at him, trying to make sense of his words. Trying to determine if this handsome man standing before her could be the same person as the lanky youth who had left years ago with dreams of sailing the world. Her mind refused to believe. If he was Cooper, that meant she was engaged to his brother. "No, you're just not remembering correctly. How could you be Cooper? He's supposed to be in England."

He stood looking at the ground, shaking his head. A glazed look of despair had settled over his features. He glanced into her eyes, then looked away with a distant stare. His fingers toyed with a loose button on his shirt. "Hannah, I'm sorry. I know you're disappointed that I'm Cooper," he said in a harsh, choked voice. "Last night Israel found the horse I rode from Charleston. After I went to bed, I started piecing things together, and then all of a sudden, I remembered."

Hannah's head ached, and she struggled to sort things out

in her murky mind. "B–but how did you get to America? Your parents are just now on their way back from searching for you over there."

His nostrils flared, and his eyes turned hard like ice. "Those men who attacked me were the same ones who kidnapped my two friends and me and forced us to work on a British ship. When it made port in Charleston, I managed to escape and brought proof that an upstanding Charleston businessman is actually a British spy. That's why those men sought to kill me. They must have thought my injuries from the fall off the horse mortal; otherwise, I've no doubt they would have put a lead ball through my heart."

Hannah pinched the bridge of her nose and pressed her eyes shut in an effort to stop the burning sensation. "So it's true then?" She opened her eyes and stared up into his sky-blue eyes, and suddenly a memory of the two little boys she used to play with flashed through her mind. Both had black hair, but one had a smattering of freckles across the bridge of his nose and. . .the bluest eyes she had ever seen. . . . They were Cooper's eyes. The older boy who filled her memory was Jamie. The two boys looked very similar, but as her memory sharpened, she suddenly knew the truth—he *was* Cooper. She recognized the tiny scar on his cheekbone from the time he swung off a rope affixed to the barn rafter and fell, scraping his face.

As the reality of the situation finally sank in, Hannah's whole body started trembling, and tears gushed forth in a torrent down her cheeks. She swayed and reached for Cooper as her knees buckled. "No, it can't be true," she whispered. "I can't be in love with my fiancé's brother."

Cooper caught her and lifted her up into his strong arms. Hannah suspected his soft grunt was both physical and emotional pain. She buried her face in his shoulder as he carried her over to a pile of hay and sat down. Holding her on his lap, he pulled her securely against his chest. Hannah tightened her grip on Cooper's shirt. How desperately she needed to cling to him. Her anguish peaked to shatter her last shred of self-control. A raw, primitive grief overwhelmed her.

How could God do this to her?

To them?

fifteen

Minutes passed as they held each other in silent sorrow. Cooper hated to move, knowing this might well be the last time he held Hannah. He finally cleared his throat and whispered against Hannah's hair, now damp with his own tears, "Angel, it doesn't change how I feel about you. I still love you more than life itself."

After a few moments, Hannah gave him a tight squeeze and lifted her head. His gut wrenched at her puffy, splotched face. Her reddened, watery blue eyes gazed deeply into his. "I knew the first time I saw your beautiful blue eyes that there was something familiar about them. I don't know why I didn't recognize them sooner, Ada—uh, Cooper."

He offered a weak smile as she stroked his cheek with her soft hand. He loved the sound of his true name on her perfectly shaped lips. Cooper's gaze caressed her face, memorizing every inch of it, knowing the days ahead would be the hardest of his life.

"Do you know what today's date is?"

"What?" She wrinkled her brow. "Oh, uh. . .yes, it's April thirtieth. Why?"

"April thirtieth?" Cooper set Hannah back. He only had two days before the *Syrius*, a British frigate posing as a French warship, would set sail again and take his two friends and the other captive Americans with it.

Early this morning he'd gone to the field where he'd hidden the pouch with the stolen documents. He forked his fingers through his hair. Whom could he turn to for help? He'd been gone for so many years that he no longer knew what men his father trusted. Who was powerful enough to stop that ship from sailing? He turned back to face Hannah. "When is your father due back?"

She dabbed her puffy red nose with an embroidered handkerchief. "I came to tell you, but I didn't get the chance. My parents returned last night."

"I've got to talk to your father right away. I need to get to Charleston by tomorrow. There's a British ship that's anchored in the harbor."

Hannah gasped. "How is that possible?"

"Because it's disguised as a French vessel, and a number of Americans who have been abducted and forced to serve as sailors are onboard it. I was one of them. I've lost so much time because of my injuries that I've got to leave today. I must talk to your father, and I need to borrow a horse."

"Oh, Coop." Hannah lightly touched his arm. "I knew in my heart that you weren't dead. We can take my buggy."

He shook his head. "I don't want you to go. Those men are still after me. They want the document I have proving what I'm saying is true."

Hannah clamped her hands to her waist. "You can't keep me from going home." Her tone held defiance as well as a subtle challenge.

He smiled at her spunk. Here was the woman he loved but could never have. He'd finally remembered why he knew what her sampler would say when completed: NEXT TO GOD, FAMILY IS MOST IMPORTANT. That motto had been drilled into him for as long as he could remember. He couldn't stand between his brother and the woman Jamie planned to marry. Cooper would sacrifice his dream so that Jamie could realize his.

He loved his brother as much as he loved Hannah. His father's own brother had hated him and nearly killed him. Lucas Reed had drilled into his sons that family comes first. Brother was loyal to brother—even if it meant sacrificing what he wanted most in this world.

He and Hannah would never have the chance to laugh together and to love each other completely. Tears burned his eyes, and he felt her loss already.

Hannah's eyes glimmered with unshed tears. "Oh Coop, what are we going to do?"

He shook his head. "I don't know, angel. I've prayed all night, ever since my memory came back. It was such a bittersweet event—to finally know who I am and yet to realize that the woman I'm in love with is promised in marriage to my own brother. The pain of it just about killed me."

Cooper ran his hand through his hair and paced back and forth in front of her.

"Let's go tell my parents what happened. Surely they'll understand."

He stopped pacing and turned toward Hannah. Her naiveté was both frustrating and enchanting. "Understand what? That you sheltered and tended a wounded stranger without any thought of your own safety? If I'd been a lesser man, I could have done horrible things to you. Are you going to tell them that you shaved me and doctored my injuries? I know it was all completely innocent, but do you honestly believe your parents will see it that way?"

Hannah's eyebrows shot upward. "You *were* injured and couldn't have hurt me if you wanted to."

Cooper couldn't hold back the bitter laugh. "Do you truly believe that? Don't you remember the day you found me in the barn when I grabbed your wrist and you couldn't pull away? And what about in the secret room when I thought you were one of my attackers, and I jerked you down into my lap? I could have overpowered you at any minute, Hannah. For a moment, when we were kissing that day, the thought actually ran through my mind. It scared me so much that I dropped you on the floor." Cooper rubbed the back of his neck. "Thank God nothing happened."

Hannah stalked toward him. "Why are you talking like this? I saved your life. There's nothing shameful about it. You would have died if I hadn't found you in the barn."

Cooper suddenly felt exhausted. What he had to tell her would drive a permanent wedge between them, but there was nothing else to be done. "Maybe it would have been for the best. I'll die bit by bit, every day, if you marry my brother."

"Stop it, Cooper," Hannah yelled. "I don't want to marry Jamie. You're the one I love." She crossed her arms over her chest. "You're scaring me."

Cooper knew the things he said had hurt Hannah, but it was the only way to make her understand the reality of the situation. "You know I said I'd marry you when I found out my true identity, but all that's changed now. I—I won't go against my own brother and steal his betrothed."

Her mouth dropped open, and she lifted her hand over her throat. Her eyes darkened with pain. "You don't mean that."

Cooper's throat ached from the thought of losing her. "Yes, I do. You're promised to Jamie. We can't go against the wishes of both our families. You have to marry my brother." He all but choked on the dreadful words. A sensation of complete loneliness and defeat engulfed him. This was his darkest hour, worse even than the day he was captured and thrown into that dark hole in the belly of that despised ship.

"I thought you loved me." Hannah's features contorted with shock and anger. Tears ran down her pale cheeks in rivers. "You're a liar! You probably said all those things just so I would take care of you and let you kiss me. How many other girls have you done that to? Oh—I hope I never see you again!" Hannah turned and ran around the side of the barn and out of sight.

Cooper stood unmoving, stunned to see his sweet angel ranting in a fit of hysteria. Had he made the wrong choice?

It had taken all night to come to his decision. Wasn't his brother's happiness, as well as that of his mother and Hannah's parents, more important than his own?

"Wait, Hannah! You know I love you," Cooper yelled, suddenly sorry for pushing her away. She couldn't hear him. Hannah was already in the buggy, racing toward the horizon.

&.

Boss watched the Madison girl drive away from the Reed house at a fast pace, and one corner of his mouth turned up. He spat out a chaw of tobacco and wiped his mouth on his sleeve before turning to his men. "See, I told you the kid would come here. Looks like that girl lied to us."

"Yeah, Boss, and it kinda looks like he ain't man enough t' handle her. I think she needs a real man."

Boss raised his hand as if he were going to smack Jeeter. "Shut up, Jeeter, and get on your horse. Sam, I'll keep an eye on the kid, and you two go catch up with the girl. Just maybe, we can use her as a bargaining chip."

&.

Could there be any hope for the two of them now? As if he could see clear to heaven, Cooper stared up at the brilliant morning sky before he left for Madison Gardens. *Why did this have to happen, God? No matter what I do, I'll hurt someone I love.*

Cooper pressed his forehead, hoping to rub away the dull, aching pain embedded there. Though he wanted nothing more than to make things right with Hannah, he wouldn't. It was best that she understand that he couldn't go against his brother, no matter what. His father's twin brother had nearly destroyed the family because of his bitterness. Lucas Reed had raised his sons to love and respect one another and to always put the other before himself. He couldn't—he wouldn't take away from Jamie the woman he was to marry.

He saddled an old mare that Israel had called Honey

and mounted. Before riding off, he took a long look at his family home. How could he have not recognized this place? How could he have forgotten that he was Cooper Reed, son of Lucas and Heather Reed, one of Charleston's most prominent couples?

When he left as a youth years ago to sail on his father's ship, he always knew he'd return one day, but now he didn't have that assurance. The best thing for everyone would be for him to disappear again. Perhaps he'd return to England and finish his education. Or perhaps he'd travel west and see some of the frontier. But first, he had to save his friends.

A short while later, he topped the tallest hill between the Reed and Madison plantations. Memories flooded back as Cooper rode up to the Madison's large house. He glanced at the big barn, shining bright with a fresh coat of white paint. He remembered playing there with Hannah, swinging on a rope, then jumping into a big pile of freshly cut hay. Hannah had sneezed and talked about the tiny specks of dust dancing on the rays of sunlight that sneaked in through cracks in the side of the barn. Fairies, she'd called them. Cooper smiled at the sweet memory.

Another image of him and Hannah hiding out in the hayloft while Jamie, Kit, and Michael searched for them rushed through his mind. His heart lurched as he remembered Hannah's sparkling eyes and mischievous grin the day she picked up an old, dried horse flop and lobbed it at Michael's head.

For a moment, Cooper wished he'd never regained his memory; then he and Hannah might have had a chance to be together. But who would have rescued his friends? He couldn't let them suffer, not as long as it was within his power to stop it, and besides, he would never have been satisfied not knowing the truth about himself. Yet now that he knew, how could he live with the pain of reality?

Cooper's thoughts drifted back to when Hannah had found him in the barn. It amazed him that he hadn't remembered her the first time he saw her. But then, she had changed—a lot. She had only been a slip of a girl about thirteen when he left. He could remember the tears in her eyes the day he rode away with his father.

He reined Honey to a stop in front of the Madisons' home. A tall, broad-shouldered man who looked to be in his early fifties, moseyed out the front door of the house. The man looked at him and touched the end of his hat. "Good day, stranger. Welcome to Madison Gardens."

"Mr. Madison?" Coop dismounted but didn't approach Hannah's father.

"Yes, I'm Richard Madison. Have we met before?"

"Yes, sir, but it's been a long time. I'm Cooper Reed."

"Cooper?" The man's mouth fell open. "Well, I'll be a hog's uncle. We all thought you were dead." Richard jogged down the steps, clapped him on the shoulders, and looked him over. "What happened to you? Where have you been?" He yanked Cooper into a hug that made his sides ache. Richard stepped back and shook his head. "Your folks sure must be relieved to know you're all right." He looked past Cooper. "Where are they? Back at Reed Springs? Caroline had hoped your mother would stop by here first, but I suppose they were anxious to get home after being away for so long."

Cooper tied the horse to a hitching post. "I haven't seen my parents since they visited me several years ago in England. I just came from Reed Springs, and they aren't there."

Richard pursed his lips. "They'll be home soon. Caroline got a letter from your mother. So. . .what happened to you? Did you know your parents have been in England, searching for you?" He chuckled and shook his head. "Won't they get the surprise of their lives." Then he scowled. "You've worried your family, son. You should have let them know you were alive and in America."

"I couldn't, sir. I ran into some trouble." Cooper shook his head. "I was abducted along with some friends back in England and forced to work on a British ship the past six months. I have to get to Charleston. There's a British ship in the harbor that has Americans aboard who've been forced to work for the British. There's a Mr. Sutherland who poses as a local businessman."

"Poses?" Richard stiffened at the mention of the name. "I know Arlis Sutherland. His daughter was just here. She's a good friend of Hannah's. Your father and I have talked about Sutherland on more than one occasion. Always thought there was something nefarious about the man."

"Could I borrow a horse, sir? This one I took from home is too old to make the journey to Charleston." Cooper flicked his hand back toward Honey.

"Of course." Richard nodded.

"Thanks. You suppose you or Michael could ride with me? I had a run-in with some men. They were after this." Cooper handed Mr. Madison the document showing Arlis Sutherland had paid the three men for capturing any number of Americans and then forcing them into service on various British ships. "I figure they're still on the lookout for me."

Richard Madison adjusted his spectacles, studied the document, then looked off in the distance for a moment before his gaze returned to Cooper. "That's a good idea. I'll send Michael along with you, and you can take Johnny, one of my workers. He's a good shot."

Cooper followed Richard to the barn. His concern for Hannah clouded his reunion with his old buddy, Michael. During the hour it took to prepare the horses and stock up on food, water, and weapons, Cooper kept watching for Hannah, wishing she'd return home. He'd wanted nothing more than to charge after her, take her in his arms, and comfort her, but he had no right to do so. The deep, twisting pain knifed his insides again.

Hannah wasn't his to love.

She belonged to his brother.

sixteen

"Simeon, please pull over. I'd like a few moments to walk by the creek."

The buggy slowed, then stopped. Simeon hurried down from his seat and helped Hannah to step out.

"I won't be long. I just need some time to walk and think. In fact, you can go on back to Reed Springs and wait for Chesny. We're close enough to home that I can make it on my own from here." Hannah turned and walked toward the creek, eager to be alone.

"Miz Hannah, Chesny wouldn't be too happy if'n I was to leave you all alone."

"I'll be fine, Simeon."

He crossed his arms over his thin chest and leaned back against one of the buggy wheels. "You go on and take yo' walk, but I be waitin' right here when yo' done."

Hannah blew out a frustrated breath and nodded. He was just trying to protect her, and that should make her feel good, but it didn't. There was only one man she wanted watching over her other than her father, and that was Cooper. But it didn't look as if that would be happening.

Her lower lip quivered. She felt exhausted, as if every shred of hope had left her. Why did she have to be the one to find Cooper? She was content to marry Jamie and hadn't questioned her arranged marriage until Ruthie came and started asking her about it and then Cooper came and stole her heart. She could have gone ahead and married Jamie and been happy, even though she didn't love him. But now that she had experienced falling in love, how could she follow through with the wedding?

She swiped her burning eyes. Pebbles crunched against her shoes, and she stopped right at the water's edge. It lapped gently against the rocks, making a soft gurgling sound. If only she were as peaceful, but instead, a war raged inside her. Hannah picked up a rock and tossed it in, feeling a bit victorious for disturbing the quiet and creating concentric circles rippling through the water. She threw in another one.

Would her mother listen to reason if Hannah explained about her love for Cooper? No, her mother was tenacious—like an alligator with its prey. Once she snagged onto an idea, there was no changing her mind. The idea for Hannah and Jamie to wed had long ago taken root in her mother's plans—and those roots ran as deep as a hickory tree's. Even if she worked up her nerve to tell her mother, Cooper had made it clear that he wouldn't stand in the way of his brother's marriage—no matter what it cost him.

Fresh tears stung her eyes. She clamped her lips together, imprisoning a sob.

Dear God, is this my fault because I'm weak? I don't understand. Father, I don't know what to do. She buried her face in her hands.

Hannah heard the sudden sound of boots scuffling on the pebbles behind her. Cooper! He'd come after her. She wiped the tears from her face and spun around. She sucked in a gasp, as a shiver of panic snaked down her spine. She stood face-to-face with two of the men who'd confronted her before.

The small man gawked at her like she was a huge steak he was ready to devour. He stepped forward, grabbing her upper arms.

"What are you doing? Let me go!" Twisting and jerking, she fought against the strong hands that held her captive. One of her arms broke free, but the other man grabbed hold of it.

The small, filthy man with rancid breath nestled up against her cheek, pricking her skin with his stubble. "Now you jes' hush up, missy, and stop yer strugglin'. Me and Sam's gonna take good care of you."

Sam. That name was familiar. Jerking her face away from his, she stared at the taller man and recognized his bushy moustache. "What do you want? My father will have your head if you don't let me go."

"Yer daddy don't scare us none, little lady," Sam growled.

"Maybe we can get the kid to swap this little gal fer that information he's got and get us a ransom out of ol' man Madison to boot." The sleazy man grinned and stroked his weak chin as if he were seeing hundreds of dollars coming his way.

Swap her? For the kid's information? What kid?

These were definitely the same men who were looking for Cooper, so he must be "the kid." Suddenly, it all made sense. They were searching for the documents he had that proved he'd been kidnapped. Somehow she had to warn him, but how could she get away from these ruffians? Simeon would help her, but if she cried out to him, her captors might shoot him. And what would they do to her? Her whole body started shaking as if she'd gotten lost in a blizzard.

"Relax, girl, nothin's gonna happen to you unless that Reed kid won't cooperate. We're just gonna take a little ride and get all of this sorted out." Sam motioned toward his horse with his head. "Get the rope, Jeeter."

Hannah clenched her eyes shut. A fear unlike any she'd ever known bore into the pit of her stomach. Her family would be distraught when she didn't return home before dark. They would all be out looking for her.

Jeeter let go of her, but Sam grabbed her around the waist with a grip as tight as iron shackles.

Moments later, the bony bandit returned with a rope.

"Stick out yer hands, missy. I jes want t' be sure you don't wander off." He ogled her face as he wrapped the prickly rope around her wrists, and his beady eyes lingered on her lips, then his gaze roved down to her chest. He licked his lips and looked up at her with a wicked grin. Her heart stopped.

"Maybe me and you'll have some fun later on tonight."

A wave of nausea churned in Hannah's stomach. A measure of fear she'd never known clung to her like burrs on stockings. The world started swaying. Suddenly Sam scooped her up and tossed her onto the back of one of the horses. He took the other end of the rope that bound her hands and tied it to the saddle horn. Then he turned around to the other man. "Jeeter, you fool. You touch this gal, and I'll kill you myself."

"Aw, cain't a man have a little fun?"

"Not with this gal."

Hannah's hopes rose ever so slightly. Perhaps God had sent Sam to watch out for her. *Thank You, Lord, for protecting me from that vile man. Give me courage. Please, God, help me to figure out some way to escape, and protect Cooper from these men who mean to do him harm.*

A short while later, as they approached the Reeds' house, the leader of the trio of outlaws rode toward them. Hannah could tell by his expression that he wasn't in a pleasant mood.

"The kid lit out of here like the barn was on fire," he said, jerking his mount to a quick halt. "I followed him over to the Madisons'. He talked with ol' man Madison; then he and two others rode out like they was headed toward Charleston. C'mon, we gotta try and catch up to 'em."

He kicked his mount hard in the sides with his heels, and the big horse bolted forward. Jeeter rode off after him, leaving a dusty cloud in his wake. Hannah grabbed the saddle horn as Sam clucked to his horse.

That evening, they approached the outskirts of Charleston.

Hoping for a chance to escape, Hannah stayed awake the whole day, waiting and watching for the perfect moment. They took back roads and trails, hugging groupings of trees that afforded cover. They rode into a part of Charleston that Hannah had never been to before.

"You two get her out of sight. I'm riding over to update Mr. S. on what all's happened." Boss rode off in another direction.

Sam and Jeeter stopped in a rank-smelling alley. Sam slid off the back of his horse, then pulled her down. He tugged her into a dirty building and shoved her into a small, dark room. Then he pulled a filthy kerchief from around his neck and gagged her.

"You keep quiet, or I'll let Jeeter in, you hear?"

Hannah nodded, fighting the urge to retch from the nasty cloth in her mouth. The door shut, taking the light with it, and she stood in the dark. All alone.

She backed up to a chair she'd noticed just before the door shut and lowered herself into it. The foul-smelling room must be used for storage. There were no windows, and she'd noticed a stack of crates along the far wall. But now, in the dark of night, she couldn't see a thing.

Desperate concern for Cooper buffeted her. She felt as if her prayers weren't reaching past the ceiling. Before long, exhaustion won out over her fear and discomfort, and Hannah turned sideways in the chair, laid her head against its back, and drifted off to sleep, dreaming of a daring rescue by the man she loved.

&

The sensation of falling jolted Hannah awake. She shoved one leg forward and caught herself before she tumbled to the floor. Staring in the inky blackness, she shook her head, trying to get her sleep-laden mind to focus on her surroundings. The horrors of the evening came rushing back.

What had her family done when she hadn't returned home? Were they out searching for her even now? Was Cooper?

Her heart ached at the very thought of him.

She might never see him again unless she got free of this place. The nasty neckerchief that had been crammed halfway down her throat to ensure her silence bit into the corners of her mouth. She lifted her hands and tried to work it free. Her shoulder muscles cramped from her wrists being bound so tightly that she could barely move.

Her nostrils flared as she labored to breathe through her nose. A strong odor assaulted her senses. At times she thought sure she wouldn't get enough air and would suffocate. Hannah leaned her head back against the rough chair and closed her eyes. *Relax. Panicking won't help.* Slowly, her breathing returned to a normal tempo.

As her physical struggles lessened, the events of the past two days came rushing back like a flash flood. She squeezed her eyes tightly shut as the familiar burning sensation returned. *Oh Adam. No, not Adam—he's Cooper Reed. Stubborn Cooper, who won't stand against his brother.*

If he loved her as much as he said, how could he refuse to put a halt to her wedding? Why did she have to fall in love with Cooper and not Jamie?

Hannah twisted her head sideways to wipe her tears on her shoulder. Was it only this morning that her world had suddenly collapsed?

❧

"You're knocking on the door of your own home?" Michael cast a sideways glance at Cooper.

"I haven't been home in over seven years. It doesn't seem right to enter without permission." With a tight fist, Cooper pounded on the door of his family's Charleston home again.

Darkness had set in, and the bells of St. Michael's church rang, heralding the nine o'clock hour. Several Negros jogged down the street in their effort to get home before curfew. The latch jiggled and then the door opened, revealing a man about Cooper's age—a man he hadn't seen before. He had hoped for someone who knew him.

"May I help you, gentlemen?" The servant eyed Cooper and the other men, but his gaze latched on to Cooper. Did the man perchance notice his resemblance to his father?

"We need to see Lucas Reed, sir. Posthaste."

The servant's chin lifted. "Mr. Reed does not normally receive guests at this late hour."

"Well, he'll see us. This is his—"

Cooper elbowed Michael in the side. "Please tell him that Michael Madison, son of Richard Madison, is here to see him. I believe he will welcome the visit."

The servant obviously recognized the name even though he didn't seem to know Michael on sight. He nodded and held out his hand, indicating for them to enter. They did so, and the servant closed the door. "Please wait here, gentlemen."

Cooper covered his mouth to hide his yawn as he watched the doorman ascend the stairs. Was his old room still the same—the bed just as comfortable? He, Michael, and Johnny had ridden all day in order to arrive before dark, but before they could retire for the night, some serious business needed to be tended to.

Michael leaned sideways. "Why'd you punch me? I was just going to tell him you live here."

"They think me dead. I want my presence to be a surprise."

"Well, they're about to get one—a pleasant one, I would venture." Michael tugged Johnny forward. "Stand in front of Coop, and let's see how long before his father notices him."

Would his father even recognize him right off? He'd last seen his parents two years ago when they'd come to England to visit him, but he'd lost significant amounts of weight after being kidnapped and then injured. And they thought him dead. He could hardly hold back the grin threatening to burst out, knowing how stunned they would be to see him again. He would even be happy to see Jamie.

That thought killed his grin. He dearly loved his brother, but he couldn't be happy about Jamie's marriage to Hannah. If only his brother didn't love her and hadn't planned to marry her most of their lives. Coop had never told Jamie that he'd always secretly cared for the spunky girl who worked so hard to keep up with the boys she associated with.

His father exited the hallway and stopped on the upstairs landing, peering down at them. Coop scooted behind Johnny, finally allowing his smile to break forth. His father looked much the same as the last time he'd seen him, expect for having a bit more gray hair. The man was still tall and broad, in the shape of a man much younger than his actual age. It was his father's penchant for working hard that kept him looking so well.

"Michael." Lucas Reed lifted his hand in greeting, then jogged down the stairs with the stuffy servant following at a more subdued pace. "So good to see you again. How are your parents faring?"

"A pleasure to see you, too, sir, and my parents are well. They've been concerned about you." Michael shook hands with Cooper's father, then motioned toward Coop and Johnny. "We have some important business, sir. This is Johnny, one of our work hands."

Lucas shook hands with Johnny, then his gaze slid past the man to Cooper and back to Michael. Disappointment swelled within Coop, but then his father's gaze jerked back to him. He studied him with a hungered look, and Coop could see hope battling the fear to believe on his father's face.

He decided to put the poor man out of his misery. "It's good to see you again, Father."

Lucas Reed's blue eyes widened and blazed with delight. "Cooper? Is it really you, my son?"

"Aye, sir, it is." His grin burst forth as he answered like his mother would have responded.

A joyous gasp spewed from his father's mouth, and then Coop was crushed in his strong arms. "Thank You, Lord, for returning my son."

Coop hugged his father and expressed his own thanks to his heavenly Father. There had been many days when he was slaving for twenty hours at a time when he wondered if he'd ever see his family again. His father finally set him back a few feet and devoured him with his moist eyes.

"We thought you were lost to us. Where have you been? Why didn't you send word that you were safe?"

"I couldn't, sir. I was abducted from London last fall and forced to serve on a British ship all these months."

The glint in his father's eyes hardened. "I knew something nefarious must have happened. There was no sign at all of you and your classmates. How is it you are here now?"

Cooper grinned, knowing his father would be proud. "We dropped anchor in Charleston Harbor, but all of us Americans and men from some other countries were locked below. They often locked me up alone because I had a tendency to sabotage things. I didn't serve all those years on your ships without learning a thing or two. After we docked, I recognized the bells of St. Michaels and knew I was home. I managed to escape."

"Well done, son." His father clapped him hard on the shoulder.

Cooper pulled the pouch from his waistband. "I also managed to find proof that a prominent American is in cahoots with the British."

Lucas scowled. "Which American? Someone I know?"

"Have a look." He held the pouch out to his father.

Lucas pursed his lips, as if preparing himself to learn of the betrayal of a close friend. He unfolded the parchment, scanned it, and his frown deepened. "Why, this is treason!"

"And kidnapping, holding a person against his will, destroying American property, and so on and so forth." Cooper's delight in revealing this information to his father knew no bounds. If not for being abducted, he would have finished his education by now and may have well returned home. He'd be happily preparing for his brother's wedding and never have fallen in love with Hannah. He released a heavy sigh, not all that sorry about the latter, but it certainly would have made his life less complicated.

"We've not much time, Father. The *Syrius*, the British frigate I was on, is scheduled to leave tomorrow. We've got to save the others who are still held captive. I regret that I was unable to set them free before escaping. I had planned to get help and then go back for them, but I had an unforeseen accident." His fingers touched the scabbed-over wound on his head, drawing his father's gaze.

Lucas brushed Coop's hair back and studied the injury. "This is at least a week old. Where have you been since then?"

Michael snorted a laugh, and Cooper sent him a mock glare. "That's the ironic thing, Father. I was found out and chase was given. I managed to get almost home to Reed Springs when my horse gave out. I was thrown over his neck, hit my head, and then the horse rolled over me. I had amnesia and just regained my memory last night. It was Michael's sister who found me in our barn." He didn't speak Hannah's name—he couldn't for fear of giving himself away.

His father wrapped an arm around him and hugged his shoulders. "Praise be to God for watching over you. I can't tell you how grieved we've all been."

Movement upstairs drew Cooper's attention. Jamie stood at the top of the stairs, staring down.

"Come and greet our visitors, son. Your future brother-in-law has arrived."

Jamie trod down the stairs, his gaze focused on Michael. "Good to see you again."

The two men shook hands.

"So, how's that sister of yours?" Jamie asked.

Michael's gaze darted to Cooper, making his heart jump. Did Michael know? He hadn't said anything about caring for Hannah, but had she talked about him to her brother?

"Uh, she's well. She's been spending a lot of time at Reed Springs, getting it ready for your return."

Jamie smiled, turning Cooper's stomach. "Good. Soon enough it will be her home, too."

His father cleared his throat and introduced Johnny. "And of course you know this young man."

Jamie lifted his gaze to Cooper, and for the first time, Coop realized he'd grown taller than his brother by a good inch and a half. The same confusion crinkled his brother's brow; then his mouth dropped, and he glanced at his father. Lucas Reed smiled broadly and nodded. Delight spread across Jamie's face. "Cooper?"

He nodded. "Aye, brother."

Jamie closed the distance between them and enveloped Cooper in a hug. "How is it you are here? Where have you been?"

Michael shook his head. "Why not send for your mother so we don't have to go through all this a third time?"

"An excellent idea." Lucas Reed grabbed Michael's shoulder and shook it. "I'll get her now. She will be so delighted." His long legs took the stairs three at a time.

Warmth flooded Coop's insides. He was finally home— with his family. Jamie shook him, regaining his attention. "It's so good to see you again, brother. You've arrived just in time for the wedding."

seventeen

A noise jerked Hannah awake again, and she was much relieved to see bright shafts of sunlight penetrating the dark room. The door opened and several men clomped in, each one looking at her. One man lit the two oil lamps hanging overhead, fully illuminating Hannah's prison for the first time since she'd arrived.

Squinting against the brightness, she slowly lifted her gaze up the length of a huge man wearing a tan coat who stood before her. He yanked down his gold vest, futilely attempting to cover his generous stomach. He doffed his black beaver hat and gave Hannah a smug smile. "Sam, untie the poor girl. Jeeter, go to the kitchen and get her some water or tea and something to eat. She must be half-starved." He smiled a grin she was certain he thought charming as Sam removed her bindings and the gag, but it sickened her stomach.

"I suggest you keep quiet, Miss Madison, unless you'd like to be gagged again."

Sam walked across the room and deposited the ropes in a box.

Hannah slowly stretched her shoulders, trying to work out the stiffness. At the moment, she couldn't have screamed even if she'd been inclined to. She desperately needed some water. She rubbed her wrists, chafed with red rope burns. Glancing up, she surreptitiously studied the big man as she moved her tongue around, trying to work up some moisture in her dry mouth. She'd seen him before, but she couldn't remember where.

The door banged opened again and that weasel of a man

returned, but this time he looked like an angel. In his hand, he carried a tin cup.

"Here's a cup of water. Lily's whipping up some grub fer the princess."

Hannah's gaze never left the cup. She licked her parched lips in anticipation. Jeeter handed it to her and turned, going back out the door. Though she wanted to gulp the cool water in one big swig, she sipped it slowly, using the extra moments to regain her composure. Anger over her abduction and concern for Cooper fueled her resolve to face the intimidating man head-on while her mind grappled for an escape plan. With a loud bang, she slammed the empty tin cup onto the table and smiled to herself when the big man jumped slightly.

"Who are you and what do you want with me?" She licked her lips to moisten them, wishing she had more water, but not wanting to lower herself to ask.

"I'm Arlis Sutherland, and I'm planning on making a little deal for myself. I'm going to trade you for some papers that were stolen from me," he said, as he lowered his enormous frame onto the chair across from her.

Hannah had a fleeting moment of pity for the poor chair as it creaked and groaned, but then his name registered, and she glanced up at him again. Ruthie's father? She'd only seen the imposing man a time or two, and even then, from a distance. Poor Ruthie. She shook her head in response to the man's comment. "Cooper will never make a deal like that. How could you possibly think you could ever get away with this kind of a scheme?"

"I've got a pretty good bargaining chip, wouldn't you say, Miss Madison?" Mr. Sutherland plopped his hat onto the table. He ran a hand through his thinning hair and gave her a tight-lipped smile. "It seems my men saw you in the arms of Mr. Reed. I figure he'd rather have his beautiful young woman back than a measly old piece of parchment."

Hannah's cheeks warmed at the thought of someone watching her and Cooper, but as her embarrassment ebbed, anger flooded in. She jumped to her feet so quickly her chair catapulted to the ground with a loud bang. Her legs threatened to buckle, and she grabbed the edge of the table for support. Leaning forward, she looked Arlis Sutherland in the eye. "You're nothin' but a lowdown coward to use a woman as a pawn. And you're dead wrong if you're think I'll let Cooper forfeit his information to you."

Mr. Sutherland didn't flinch at her tirade. The only indication that he'd even noticed was an uplifted eyebrow. "Sit down, Miss Madison, and I suggest you quiet down," he said as he lifted up the filthy neckerchief that had been in her mouth and twirled it around his plump fingers. He flicked a finger at Boss, who strode over, and pressed her back in her seat.

"You know, my dear, you're the one who is dead wrong. But at least you're not dead yet. And to tell the truth, there are things worse than death for a beautiful young lady like you." He rubbed his generous lips with a fat finger as he gazed at her.

Hannah shrank back in her seat, suddenly realizing how much danger she was in.

Jeeter bustled back into the room and set another cup of water and a plate of greasy food in front of her. Her mouth watered, but her mind refused to acknowledge that the stuff on the plate could actually be consumable.

"Mr. Sutherland," Jeeter said with a huff. "That Reed kid's in town. He's stayin' at his family's town home."

Cooper. Hannah's gaze switched to Jeeter. Cooper was in Charleston? *Keep him safe, Lord, and please help me.*

"Did he see you?" Mr. Sutherland asked.

"Naw, he was too busy stuffin' his face and talkin' to his folks."

Arlis Sutherland scowled. "I'm done for if Lucas Reed learns that I was involved in the kidnapping of his son. Perhaps it's time I cut my losses and return to England." He picked up his hat and twirled it on his finger. "But not before I get those documents back. Here's what we're going to do. . . ."

❧

Cooper stretched his arms and then patted his belly after the delicious meal the family cook had prepared. He dabbed his lips with a cloth napkin.

"Father shouldn't be gone long," Jamie said, from across the table. "He wanted to visit several men among the leadership of Charleston to decide what charges to bring against Mr. Sutherland and how they want to handle his arrest."

Cooper had hoped to go along with his father, but his mother wouldn't let him out of her sight. She sat beside him, reaching out and patting his arm every few minutes as if to check to see if he were real.

"I'm so thankful to our Lord for your return. We only got back from England yesterday. I wanted to stay and search for you longer, but we needed to get back for Jamie's wedding." She smiled at Jamie, then patted Cooper again. "And now we'll have the added delight of you being there as well. We planned to rest up a few days before returning to Reed Springs."

Cooper fiddled with his spoon. How could he attend that wedding, knowing the only woman he ever loved would be lost to him forever? Somehow he'd have to get out of going.

Michael shoved back his chair and stood. "Thank you for the fine meal, Mrs. Reed. If you don't mind, ma'am, Johnny and I will head to our rooms and let your family visit. I know it's been a long while since you've seen that scalawag." He winked at Cooper and grinned a smile so similar to Hannah's that it made Cooper's heart clench.

His mother nodded at Michael. "I can't thank you enough for accompanying Cooper home. We're forever in your debt."

"I do believe that lemon pudding you served erased any debts, ma'am." The two men left the room.

"It's good to see Michael again. Hard to believe he'll be family soon." Jamie lifted his cup of tea and took a sip.

Cooper grimaced. He didn't want to hear anything about wedding plans. They only emphasized how much he was sacrificing for his brother's happiness. He turned away, studying the room for any changes that had been made since he was last home. Other than two new paintings, everything was just as he remembered.

His mother turned in her chair, her brown eyes shining. Tufts of gray and brown hair stuck out from under her cap. Tiny lines creased the corner of her eyes. She was aging, but she was still beautiful.

"Tomorrow, we'll go out and get you fitted for a new coat and trousers. There's just barely enough time to have some clothes made before the wedding." She cocked her head and brushed a lock of hair from his forehead. "My boy is now a man. We've all missed you so much, and we feared you were dea—" She choked on the last word and turned away.

Jamie watched her with a concerned gaze. "I told you Coop was tough, Mum. I knew in my heart he wasn't gone." He shot a grin at Cooper.

Jamie had always been the perfect big brother. Yes, he sometimes was a tease but never in a cruel manner. He was always someone Coop looked up to. Jamie always stood up for him, and never let anyone bully him. He'd grown up to be a kind, responsible man, as far as Coop could tell. He'd make a good husband for Hannah. Cooper's stomach churned. If he couldn't have her himself, there was no other person in the world he'd want caring for her other than

Jamie. At least he had that consolation.

"Why are you so down in the dumps, little brother?" Jamie's concerned blue eyes now focused on him.

Because I'm in love with your fiancée, he longed to shout. Instead, he shrugged. "Just tired, I suppose—and curious as to what Father is finding out."

"We'll know soon enough." Jamie's dark brows dipped. "It's difficult to believe Mr. Sutherland could be a British loyalist working right under our noses. Why, I do business with him on a regular basis." He pursed his lips tightly. "And to think he had my own brother locked up on one of his ships. It makes me want to—"

Their mother lifted a hand. "Remember, son, we're Christian folk. Your father and his associates will see that Mr. Sutherland is punished for his deeds, but we are to forgive."

Jamie shook his head. "How do you forgive someone for imprisoning your own son?"

"We do as God did. His Son was also imprisoned, but even Jesus forgave those who locked Him up and cruelly mistreated Him. We can do no less."

Jamie cast Coop an I'm-not-so-sure-I-can-do-that look. It warmed him that his brother would be so adamant in wanting retribution from the man who was responsible for Cooper's anguish, but his mother was right. He'd realized that no man could control life, other than in the choices he made. Life and death were in God's hands. There had been many times Coop thought he wouldn't see the light of day again, but God had brought him through, even when he didn't acknowledge God's hand in his life. "Mother is correct, Jamie. We must let go of our anger and desire for revenge. It only hurts us and those closest to us."

Jamie stared at him with his mouth partially open; then he smiled. "And when did you find God, little brother?"

"When I was locked up in a deep, dark hole, injured

and alone." They didn't need to know that hole had been at Reed Springs and not onboard the *Syrius*. All that truly mattered was that he'd reconciled with God. Something he should have done many years ago.

The front door opened and shut, and all eyes turned toward the doorway. Coop's heart jumped when his father strode in, looking confident. His gaze latched onto Coop's and he nodded.

"All is taken care of. Members of the City Guard have been dispatched to arrest Arlis Sutherland." He pulled out his chair and dropped into it.

"What about the men still held captive?"

His mother waved to a servant, who silently stood in the corner by the dining room entrance. "Please bring Mr. Reed a hot cup of tea and a bowl of pudding." She turned her eyes to her husband. "And what of Mrs. Sutherland and Ruthie? All of this will be so hard on them."

Lucas Reed pursed his lips and shook his head. "I know not what will happen to them. I suppose they will return to England. Life will certainly be difficult if they choose to remain in Charleston."

"Yes, I'm sure it will."

Coop thought of the arrogant young woman he'd met the day Hannah found him. She would certainly be brought down from the high horse she was on. Being the daughter of a traitor would forever tarnish her life.

Coop listened to his family talk and studied each face. Once Jamie married Hannah, she would sit at the family's table. How could he endure that?

He clenched his jaw. He couldn't. And it wouldn't be fair to her to have him present. No, the best thing for everyone would be for him to leave again—the best for everyone, that is, but himself.

eighteen

"I don't know why you think I need so many clothes, Mother." Cooper shook his head as he thought of all she had ordered for him at the four shops that they'd just visited. It was enough for three men.

"Because you are returning to society, and you have nothing but the clothes on your back."

"And those are mine." Jamie grinned widely.

Cooper couldn't very well explain he'd never use most of those clothes since he'd be leaving soon.

"Why don't we take luncheon at McCradys?" His mother tugged his arm, and he turned, allowing her to guide him toward the tavern well known for its fine food.

Cooper's forward progress halted when he came to a man leaning back in a chair. His crossed arms lay on his chest and his feet rested on the handrail, blocking the walkway. The man's face was hidden beneath his black hat.

"Excuse me, mister," Cooper said.

He pushed back his hat and looked up at him with a steely gaze.

Cooper took a step back, bumping into his brother. "That's one of the men who attacked me," he whispered over his shoulder to Jamie. Turning back to the man, Cooper's heart skipped a beat when he saw a gun pointed at his chest. His hand edged ever so slowly toward the knife hanging under his shirt.

His mother gasped, and she backed up, running into Jamie. "What do you want with us?"

The man with the droopy moustache jumped to his feet, ignoring Cooper's mother. "So you remember me, huh, kid?"

His gaze dropped to Cooper's hand. "Git that hand away from that gun and keep 'em where I can see 'em."

"I don't have a gun," Coop said.

"Look. . ." Jamie set their mother behind him and stepped forward. "We don't want any trouble."

"Well, seems to me you've got it whether you want it or not," boomed a deep voice behind them.

Cooper spun around just as Jamie and their mother did. Two more men with guns had sneaked up behind them. Cooper glanced around but knew that no one had noticed their predicament.

"Let's just take a little walk that way." The biggest man said as he waved his gun toward the alley.

"What makes you think we'll go anywhere with you?" Jamie challenged. "There are people everywhere. Somebody will see you and know you're holding us against our will. The City Guard's office is just down the street."

The man sneered. "Go ahead and holler, but there's a pretty little gal that just might like to see y'all first."

Cooper felt the skin on his face tighten at the man's declaration.

"What girl is he talking about?" his mother asked, turning to gaze at him.

Cooper looked at her. He closed his eyes and sucked in a deep breath. *Oh God, take care of Hannah. This is all my fault. I shouldn't have let her ride off alone when she was so upset.* With resolve, he turned to Jamie. "They must have Hannah."

"Hannah? What does she have to do with this?" Jamie narrowed his eyes as he stared at Cooper. Though he wanted to slink away like a dog who'd stolen the steak off his master's plate, Cooper held his brother's gaze.

"So y'all coming or not?"

Jamie silently nodded, finally breaking his gaze. In unison, they turned in the direction the big man's gun waved and followed the man who had been sitting in the chair.

❧

Hannah jumped when the door banged open again. Her abductors had returned bringing some more people with them. She sighed. With a room full of captors, there'd be no chance for her escape.

The small room began to fill with people. One, two. . .five people walked in. Her breath caught in her throat as she recognized Cooper's lean form coming through the door. *No, Lord, not Cooper, too.* Sam held a gun to his back. Hannah looked up to meet Cooper's gaze, and she saw the regret encompassing his handsome face.

"Sit down," Arlis Sutherland ordered as he stood, his chair squeaking as if happy to be relieved of its monstrous burden. He motioned a hand to the only woman in the group, and as she stepped out from behind Cooper, Hannah realized it was her future mother-in-law, Heather Reed. She walked over and sat in the chair Mr. Sutherland had just occupied. Mrs. Reed offered Hannah a soft smile and reached out, grasping her hands. She was grateful for the silent support.

Cooper sat on the edge of the desk, next to Hannah. He subtly reached a hand behind her and briefly patted her back. Warmth traveled up her spine, and it took all the restraint she could muster not to jump into his arms.

Hannah glanced up, expecting to see Lucas Reed, but instead, her gaze collided with Jamie's. He walked over and stood behind her chair and his mother's. Heather glanced over her shoulder into Jamie Reed's eyes. He offered her a reassuring smile, then cast a peculiar glance in his brother's direction.

"Now, I want to know where my papers are." Mr. Sutherland smacked his meaty fist on the table near Heather Reed, and she jumped and leaned back, eyes wide.

"You're too late," Jamie told him, the timbre of his voice

sounding much like Coop's.

"What do you mean?"

"My father and a number of his associates have already seen the information," Cooper said.

Ppffp! Sutherland exhaled a loud breath, which sounded to Hannah as if he practically strangled on it. "You're lying!"

"No, we're not. Evidently you haven't been home or you would have already been arrested." Cooper lifted his chin in the air. "So you see, you're too late. By now the captive sailors have been set free. You're a wanted man, Mr. Sutherland."

Ruthie's father stood glaring at him. Turbulent emotions flashed across his thick face, and his gray eyes darkened like angry thunderclouds. He turned his gaze on Hannah, and she became increasingly uneasy under his scrutiny. "Well, in that case, I may need a hostage to insure my safety. Sam, get the girl."

Hannah flinched at the icy tone of his voice. She felt the nauseating sinking of despair, and she bit her lip until it throbbed like her pulse. Feeling like a trapped animal, she looked at Cooper and then over to Jamie and Sam, who hadn't yet moved. Suddenly, Cooper jumped to his feet, but Jeeter jammed his pistol into his back and growled, "Sit down, sonny, 'fore I knock ya in the head with my gun like I did before."

Sam crossed the room in three steps and moved in Hannah's direction before a knock on the door halted him. He turned to Mr. Sutherland, who nodded for him to answer.

"Who's there?"

"It's me, Lily. Jeeter said I was to bring some more water and some whiskey."

Sam looked at Mr. Sutherland. He nodded again. Hannah thought Mr. Sutherland probably reasoned he needed a drink about now. She exhaled a sigh, glad for the short reprieve, and shot another prayer heavenward.

Sam opened the door just wide enough to slip his slim

body through, then pulled the door shut behind him. Moments later, the door burst open. The room instantly filled with people with guns drawn. Jeeter's flintlock boomed behind her, and Hannah jerked her head down. The doorjamb splintered into tiny fragments just inches from her father's head. Jamie leaped from his chair. With the strength of youth behind him, he wrestled away the pistol Arlis Sutherland had just pulled from his waistband. As if blasted with a stick of dynamite, Cooper flew off the desk and knocked Jeeter to the floor. Boss cowered in the corner, eyes wide, anger battling with defeat. Several members of the City Guard strode over and quickly took Boss into custody.

Hannah massaged her ears with her fingertips and opened her mouth wide in hopes of clearing the ringing. The acrid odor of gunpowder stung her eyes. She looked over at Heather Reed. The older woman sat with her hands over her face. Wide brown eyes peered over her fingertips.

"Hello, Sutherland. Seems you have something that belongs to me," Richard Madison seethed through clenched teeth. He strode over and grabbed Sutherland by his cummerbund.

Michael stepped into the doorway with his gun ready and surveyed the scene. Buster slipped in behind him and went to stand protectively next to Hannah. He growled a low snarl and took a step toward Jeeter, who still wrestled with Cooper on the floor near Hannah's feet. Boots scraped against the wooden floor as the two men struggled. At the sight of the large dog's bared teeth near his face, Jeeter's spirit seemed to wither. In a matter of seconds, Cooper had the man on his feet with the gun now in his back.

"Well, Arlis, it looks to me like you're a bit outnumbered. What do you suppose we should do about it?" Hannah's father asked.

Arlis Sutherland scanned the room. The defeat registered on his face. "I fail to see that I have a say in the matter."

He knocked his former business associate's hand off his cummerbund, and his large body hunkered down on the only empty chair in the room.

Richard Madison holstered his pistol and turned toward Hannah. "Are you all right, princess?"

Hannah jumped up and threw her arms around him. "Yes, Papa, but I was so scared for a while. I thought for sure they were going to take me away and I'd never see you again. How did you ever find me?"

"We had the good Lord's help, your mother's prayers, and a little bit of luck. Seems Jason Mayburn was riding out to talk to me about borrowing the services of my new bull. When he arrived, we were all half-crazy from looking for you. You'd been gone all day and it was getting dark and nobody had seen you. Mayburn mentioned that he passed three people, two men and a woman, on his way to Madison Gardens. He said the woman resembled you and didn't look too happy. So we packed up and made a beeline to town. Buster was the one that tracked you down once we got here. I guess you owe that ol' dog a big bone."

Hannah knelt down and gave Buster a big hug. He plastered a wet, sloppy kiss on her face. "Eeww!"

The tension broke around the room as everyone, except for the prisoners, started laughing. The City Guard members who'd been waiting outside, guarding Sam, left to escort the four men to jail.

"Richard, thank you so much for rescuing us." Mrs. Reed stood and hurried to his side. "I suppose you've heard that Cooper has been returned to us."

His smile stretched from ear to ear. "Yes, he borrowed a horse and my son."

"We can't thank you enough for your help." Mrs. Reed brushed the hair back from Hannah's face. "Are you all right, dear?"

Hannah smiled. "Yes, thank you."

"Well, I would imagine you'd like to get out of here."

She nodded. "That I would, most certainly. I'm famished."

Heather nodded to Jamie. "Wouldn't you care to escort your fiancée, son?"

Jamie slipped past Cooper. "Yes, ma'am, I would."

Hannah darted a glance at Cooper, who matched her strained smile with his own weak one. Her heart skipped like a ricocheting lead ball.

"Might I have the pleasure?" Jamie stepped toward her, and she looked up at him with effort. He reached for his hat and seemed to realize it was gone. He turned and searched the floor.

"Looking for this?" Michael grinned as he handed Jamie a smashed black hat. Jamie took it and fluffed it and pressed it onto his thatch of dark hair. He turned back to Hannah and gave a smile so like Cooper's that Hannah wanted to cry.

"You've grown up to be quite a beauty, Miss Hannah."

She cleared her throat and felt her cheeks flush. She peeked around Jamie's arm and over at Cooper. He scowled at his brother's back, then shoved his hands to his hips, and his shoulders slumped as he stared at the floor. The aching in Hannah's heart became a fiery gnawing.

"We were headed over to McGrady's to dine. Might I have the pleasure of your company as we walk there?" Hannah forced her gaze away from the man she was in love with and turned her attention on the man she would be marrying. She nodded and hesitantly slipped her hand in the crook of his arm, flashing Cooper an apologetic glance. She knew he was just as displeased with the situation as she, but now wasn't the time for a confrontation.

"Heather, if you don't mind enduring my company until that rascally husband of yours can join us. . ." Hannah's father offered his arm to Mrs. Reed.

"It would be my pleasure, kind sir."

Hannah saw Michael flash a teasing grin at Cooper and offer him his arm. Cooper scowled at him and stalked out the door alone.

"What do you suppose has gotten into him?" Mrs. Reed asked.

nineteen

This is my wedding day. Hannah exhaled a heavy sigh and stared out her bedroom window at the gray, dismal morning, which mirrored her emotions. The threat of a spring thunderstorm hung heavily in the air, every bit as foreboding as Hannah's feelings about today's event. This should have been the happiest day of her life, but she felt as if she were going to her own funeral rather than her wedding.

Cooper had avoided her ever since her rescue and his family's return to Reed Springs. Hannah knew he was hurting as much as she, but she also knew that she had to see him one last time. Once her decision was made, Hannah dressed hastily, hoping to get out of the house before her mother awoke. She pulled on a gown and tied a blue sash around the high waistline. Cooper had commented once that the ribbon brought out the color of her beautiful eyes. Her chin wobbled, and she let out a strangled gasp as tears blurred her vision. *I wonder if Jamie even knows the color of my eyes.*

Hannah collapsed on her bed and cried out loud to God. "Oh Lord, am I doing the right thing in honoring my parents' wishes and marrying Jamie? 'Delight thyself also in the Lord: and he shall give thee the desires of thine heart'—that's what Your Word says. I've been doin' my best to take delight in You. But how can I marry Jamie when I know my heart will always belong to Cooper?" She pulled a handkerchief from the dwindling stack she'd set on the table next to her bed the night before and blew her nose. "I tried to talk to Mama, but she insists she and Papa must not go back on their word to Jamie and his parents. Is that more important than their own daughter's happiness? Oh, it's all so confusing."

She allowed herself only a few moments to pour out her heart before God, then got up from her bed with resolve. If she was going to have any chance of getting away and seeing Cooper, she'd best get going now before everyone else got up. She put on her shoes and tiptoed as quietly as she could down the long hall. The clicking of her heels resonating against the wooden floor was deafening in her ears. If her shoes didn't give her away, surely the roar of her beating heart would.

Hannah tiptoed into the empty kitchen. Evidence that her mother was up and had already begun baking was everywhere. She sighed, thankful that her mother wasn't in the room just then. As she was relishing in the success of her escape, her mother came barreling in the back door, carrying a pail of eggs. Hannah's heart sank all the way down to her toes.

"You're up early on your wedding day. I suppose you're a bit anxious." Her mother huffed a laugh and set the bucket on the table. "I know I sure was the day I married your father."

Anxious, yes, but not in the same way her mother meant. "I want to go for a short walk before things get hopping around here."

"Taking a walk around your home for the last time before you marry is a grand idea. It's a good way to say good-bye to your past and to embrace your future. But then it's not like you won't be coming back often. It's only a brief walk from Reed Springs."

"I—I should go before time gets away from me."

The door banged again, and Chesny entered, carrying a pail of frothy milk. She cast a tight-lipped glance at Hannah. "Smile, child. It's yo' weddin' day!"

Was everyone against her?

Her mother nodded. "Jamie is a good man and handsome,

too. He'll make you a fine husband."

Hannah gave the women a weak smile and ran out the door just in time to hide the tears that gushed forth again. Buster fell into step beside her, and she patted his big head, welcoming his company. The mile-long walk did little to calm her turbulent emotions. In the back of her mind, she could feel God's gentle encouragements. . . . *"Trust Me".* . . . *"Trust Me."* But it was so hard to trust Him when there seemed to be no possible way out of her unwanted marriage.

As Hannah crested the last hill, the sun peeked through a break in the clouds on the horizon. Things were still quiet at Reed Springs. It looked as though everyone was still asleep, but she doubted that was true.

Hannah's eyes were glued to the house in hopes of catching Cooper alone. A movement in the corner of her eye drew her gaze to the opening barn door. Cooper walked out and looked around, as if he sensed her presence. Buster whined when he saw him.

She lifted two fingers to her mouth and blew out a whistle she'd perfected as a child, and her dog added a bark. Cooper's head jerked toward her, and their eyes met over the distance. He slowly raised his hand in acknowledgment, held it there for a moment, then disappeared back into the barn.

Heart plummeting all the way down to her boot tips, she turned back toward home. "Well, that's it, boy." She pressed Buster's head against her skirt, needing the love she knew he'd give her. Her lower lip trembled, and tears welled in her eyes. "Cooper won't talk with me."

She sighed a loud breath, determined to do what everyone expected of her, and continued walking. In a matter of hours, she'd be living at Reed Springs with Jamie, his parents. . .and Cooper. She shook that image from her mind. She had to put Cooper Reed out of her thoughts. It seemed that he had already done so with her. With resolve, she headed back to prepare for her wedding.

The *clip-clop* of quickly approaching hoofbeats stopped her dead in her tracks. She whirled around just as Cooper rode up on a gray horse that she hadn't seen before. The big animal nickered to her. . .and that was more than Cooper did. He jumped down to the ground and stood looking at her with a hard, unreadable expression on his handsome face.

She tried to hide her misery from his probing stare. Her newly found resolution melted in his presence. "Cooper— please—won't you do something to stop this?" Hannah reached out to touch his arm.

"There's nothing to be done." He stared at her with a hard, steely gaze. The blue eyes she loved so much now filled her with icy apprehension. "You want me to tell my own brother that I fell in love with the woman he's going to marry?"

"Yes!" That didn't sound so unreasonable to her.

"I—I can't. You don't understand how things are with us. Jamie and I are close. All our lives our father pounded into us that next to God, family is most important."

Hannah felt her heart shrivel as he recited the very words on her sampler—words she'd heard his father say.

"My father's brother nearly destroyed the whole family with his hate and vendetta to obliterate all that my father loved. I won't be like my uncle and cause a rift in my family—not even for you, angel. I can't do it."

The tiny spark of hope she'd managed to salvage was quickly stamped out. "But you're willing to destroy what we could have?"

Cooper looked at her through half-opened eyes. His pain-filled expression resembled someone's who'd been gut shot. "Hannah, I know I shouldn't say this, but I'll always love you. Nothing can destroy that." He looked away, his lips pressed tightly together, then he shook his head. "I'm sure I'll never marry, because no woman could ever replace you in my heart."

The ache in her heart became a fiery gnawing. "That's so easy for you to say." Hannah grabbed Cooper's upper arms and shook him with all her might. She wasn't ready to give in yet. "But what about me? You'd let me marry your brother, live in the same house, and sleep under the same roof as you, knowing that it's you I love and not him? Is that fair to Jamie?"

He heaved a sigh. "I'm leaving. . .after the wedding."

The anguish in his voice cut her to the quick. She couldn't bear the thought of never seeing him again—of being the one to drive him away from his close-knit family. "No, Cooper. . .please don't." She closed her eyes, utterly miserable, and tightened her grip on his arms to keep from falling from the weight of her despair.

When she finally reopened them, Hannah saw the tears Cooper had fought so hard against come rolling down his tan cheeks. "You're right. I can't stand the thought of you in Jamie's arms, much less sharing his bed—and me in the adjoining room. It would kill us both. Don't you see? Leaving is the only way."

"We could go away together."

"No, angel, I can't take you from your home—your family. I know how awful that can be. Besides, you know we'd be miserable if we did that." Cooper closed his eyes and shook his head. The agony on his handsome face ripped Hannah's heart in two.

"You know, it's really odd. Jamie was always the one who had to have his hands in every aspect of the shipping business, just like Father. I loved sailing, but what I'd learned during my years at sea was that I truly loved the land. I went to England to finish my education with the idea of coming back to the plantation and improving its output—of trying new things. Jamie prefers city life to living here. I'd hoped Reed Springs might be my inheritance while Jamie got the

Charleston house and the shipping business." He shoved his hands to his hips, and his shoulders hunched forward.

"So, that's it then. You're not goin' to do a thing to stop this?" she squeaked, as a suffocating sensation tightened her throat.

"I won't go against my brother. I love him too much."

Hannah covered her face with trembling hands and gave vent to the agony of her loss. "I—I guess you love him more than me then." She sobbed a strangled gasp and turned away, no longer able to look on his handsome face.

❧

Hannah's gut-wrenching plea tore at every part of his being. Cooper had gone over and over the whole situation in his head. He'd prayed for days and still had no answer. "*Trust Me*" was the message that kept coming to his mind. And he was trying to trust God. . .but there just seemed no way for this situation to turn out good for everyone.

"Hannah, please don't go like this," he said, his voice ragged.

She whipped around, throwing sharp blue daggers at him with her eyes. "Just how would you like me to be going?"

Cooper removed his tricorn and crunched the edges in his hand. He had to help her see how he felt. "I was hoping you would understand. You have two brothers. What if the situation was reversed? Could you walk in and steal Michael's intended away from him, knowing how much pain it would cause him?"

The struggle taking place on her beautiful face shredded his already battered heart. After a moment she dropped her gaze to the ground. "No, I don't suppose I could."

He lifted her chin with his finger. With the back of his hand, he wiped the tears blurring his vision, then he stood memorizing every inch of her lovely face for the last time. Tears flowed freely down both of their faces. Cooper expelled a savage groan and pulled her into his arms.

For the moment, nothing else existed. He clung to her, knowing it would be his last chance. After this moment they wouldn't belong to one another ever again.

After a few short moments, Cooper released his death grip on Hannah and tilted her face up to his. He cradled her head in his hands and his fingers entwined in her hair. "I'll love you forever, my sweet angel." He leaned down and sealed their destiny with a final kiss as their lips and tears mingled together.

All too soon, he pulled back. "Good-bye, my love, my angel." He stroked her golden tresses for the final time, then released her so fast that she stumbled. He picked his hat off the ground where he had dropped it and slapped it back onto his head. Quickly, he turned, jumped on his horse, and rode away before he changed his mind.

At least Jamie would be happy, though he would never know the sacrifice that Cooper had made.

જ

Feeling more miserable than she ever had in her twenty years, Hannah turned and slowly walked back home. Lifting the skirt of her dress, she dried her tears. It was time she prepared to become the wife of Jamie Reed.

twenty

The wedding was to take place at noon in the grassy area north of the Madisons' house, weather permitting. The menacing, gray storm clouds had threatened to release their bounty but so far had not followed through.

Hannah held up her small mirror and tried to see how her mother's wedding dress looked on her. They had taken it up in the bust and sides and let out the hem a full two inches. She despised the tightly laced corset she had to wear in order to fit into the gown's clinging bodice that tapered down to her waist. The corset made it hard to breathe and required her to stand up so much straighter than she had to when wearing her looser-fitting, high-waisted gowns. But she had to admit the royal blue dress with ecru lace trim was truly beautiful and the narrow cut made her look much slimmer.

She set the mirror on the dresser and walked over to the small window in her bedroom. Jamie and his mother were riding over the ridge in a buggy and heading toward the house, with his father riding alongside on his horse.

"Lord, I want to do Your will and to please You. Help me to be a good wife to Jamie. Perhaps in time, I'll grow to love him. I truly hope I do, for his sake. I'm going to trust You. . . trust that You have good things planned for me. Please ease this horrible pain in my heart, and take care of Cooper."

Hannah opened the large Madison family Bible and ran her finger over the page that held her family tree. After today, Jamie's name would be entered onto it next to hers. She let out a sigh and flipped the pages to Proverbs 3:5 and began reading. " 'Trust in the Lord with all thine heart;

and lean not unto thine own understanding. In all thy ways acknowledge him, and he shall direct thy paths.' Amen, Lord. That is my prayer."

"Aren't you the pretty one? Look what I have for your hair," said her mother as she burst into the room and proudly held up a chain of tiny purple violets.

"They're very pretty."

Her mother had already arranged Hannah's hair in loose curls on the back of her head with shorter curls framing her face and now placed the floral chain on her head. Hannah picked up the mirror and stared at her reflection again. The dainty flowers added a touch of femininity. "I hope Jamie will like them."

"Jamie will be so proud of you, my sweet girl, but I'll dearly miss seeing you each morning."

"As you said before, I won't be all that far away. I'm sure I'll see you most days."

Her mother patted the bed. "Come and sit beside me for a moment."

Hannah lowered herself down next to her mother. Carefully she straightened her dress, knowing the warm, moist air would instantly cause wrinkles if she sat on it wrong.

Her mother reached for her hand. "I'm so proud of you, my dear. I've looked forward to this day almost since the day you were born. Heather came to visit me a few days later and brought the boys. Jamie begged to hold you and wouldn't take no for an answer. It was so out of character for him that Heather and I joked about you two getting married when you grew up, and before long, it became our dream. I'm so happy I lived to see this day. My own mother died before I married, and I so wished she could have been at my wedding."

Hannah was dumbfounded. Her mother had never told

her that. She was destined almost from the day she was born to be Jamie's wife. This path had been laid out her whole life. She had only to follow it and everything would work out. She had to believe that.

Her mother squeezed her hand. "I saw Jamie arriving before I came in. I suppose it's time we were heading to the parlor to await the signal for the wedding to begin."

Footsteps came their way down the hall, and they both looked up. Jane appeared in the doorway. Hannah smiled at her sister.

"I've finished feeding the children and put them down for their naps. Jamie is here, and everyone is assembled." Jane crossed the room and reached for Hannah's hand, pulling her to her feet. "And don't you look lovely. Mama's dress fits you so much better than it did me."

"That's not true. I'm too tall to do it justice."

"It looked lovely on both of you, so enough of that talk. Let's be going." Her mother extended her hand toward the doorway.

Jane clapped her hands, a smile lighting her face. "Oh, did I tell you that the minister from town brought his brother? He'll be playing his violin as you march in. Won't it be so grand to have music at the wedding!"

"Yes, it's wonderful." Hannah tried to work up some enthusiasm for her sister's and mother's sake.

Jane waved them from the room. "We'd best be going."

Hannah nodded and her mother took her in her arms. As they parted, Mama wiped a tear off Hannah's cheek.

"I always cry at weddings, too." Her mother smiled and patted Hannah's cheek. "Time to be going, dear."

Taking a calming breath, Hannah followed her mother down the hall. *Go ahead and cry, Mama, and so will I, but we're not crying for the same reason.*

Moments later, Hannah peeked out the front door and

surveyed the small crowd of guests gathered around the garden entrance. Her father strode proudly toward her, a big smile on his face. Michael, deep in an animated conversation with Jamie, flung his arms out to the side. Chesny stood with the other family servants in the shade of a huge pine tree, her hands also moving quickly as she conversed with Maisy and Leta. The minister's wife stood next to Heather Reed, who also took advantage of the shade. But where was Cooper? As much as Hannah wanted him to be there, she wondered if it might be easier if he weren't.

"Are you ready to be married, daughter?" Richard Madison bellowed proudly.

"Yes, Father." *But not to the man of my choosing—not to the man who stole my heart.*

He held out his elbow to her. "Then grab hold, and let's go get you married."

Together they walked arm in arm across the porch and down the steps. Mama followed, happily humming behind them. Hannah could faintly hear the violin playing, but most of the sweet music floated away on the stiff breeze. Everyone smiled as they moved toward them. Everyone, except Cooper. Dressed in his dark church clothes and leaning against a tall oak tree, he looked as handsome as she'd ever seen him. His black tricorn was pulled down low, hiding his eyes, and his arms were crossed stiffly. The toe of his boot stirred up tiny clouds of dust that quickly floated away on the wind.

As they came closer to the small cluster of people, Jamie walked away from Michael and went to stand in front of the minister. Cooper pushed away from the tree and walked over, standing a few yards away, to the right of Michael. Hannah glanced in his direction, but his head remained downcast.

She felt her father handing her off to Jamie, and she trembled as he took her hand. Hannah looked into the lightly tanned face of the man who would soon be her husband. His Reed-blue eyes held a mischievous glint that gave her pause.

Numbness filled her whole being. The minister was saying something about the sanctity of marriage. . .leaving your father and mother and cleaving to one another. Then he said, "If any of you know cause, or just impediment, why these two persons should not be joined together in holy matrimony, please speak up now or forever hold your peace."

Except for the birds mocking her with their cheerful songs and the trees rustling in the breeze, all was quiet. Hannah glanced over her shoulder and saw Cooper standing with his hands on his hips, squirming. When he looked up and held her gaze, a tiny spark of hope flickered deep within her. His dark brows knitted together, and Hannah watched the rise and fall of his chest as he seemed to be wrestling with his thoughts.

I love you. Hannah hoped Cooper could read the silent message in her gaze.

A blazing light ignited in his blue eyes. Like a tiny flame sparking a prairie fire, suddenly his countenance changed from despair to resolve. He straightened and walked toward her.

Oh please, Lord, let it be.

Cooper stopped behind her, and the heat from his body sent goose bumps racing up her arms. "I object, Reverend."

Hannah dared to breathe again. Tears of joy blurred her vision when Cooper pushed his way between her and Jamie, ripping her hand away from Jamie's.

"I tried," he whispered, "but I just can't let you go, angel."

A cry of relief broke from her lips, and tears cascaded down her cheeks. For the first time in days, Hannah reveled in the joy of Cooper's love.

"Um-hum." The sound of Jamie clearing his throat jolted Hannah back to reality. She clung to Cooper's hand and glanced up at his brother. Even though her heart burst with joy, she desperately hoped he wouldn't be hurt. Immense relief flooded her to see his big grin. Jamie slapped Cooper on the shoulder. "It's about time you came to your senses, little brother."

Richard Madison marched up to them. "Just what is the meaning of all this?"

"Well, sir, it seems my little brother just about made the biggest mistake of his life," Jamie said.

"What mistake?" Lucas Reed roared.

"Don't know why you couldn't see it, Father." Jamie interrupted. "You and Mother were so busy tryin' to marry me off to Hannah that you were blind to the fact that she doesn't love me. She's in love with Cooper."

"How can she be in love with Cooper? She hasn't seen him since she was young." Heather Reed rose from her chair and stood next to Jamie.

"Well, Mum," Jamie said, "it seems that my little brother stole my intended right out from under my nose."

Clinging to Cooper's strong hand with both of hers, Hannah dared a glance at Jamie's face. He looked as relieved as she felt. Had he, too, been forced into this near-marriage? She'd thought he wanted to marry her, but perhaps he was just as apprehensive. She thought sure her heart would explode any second with sheer joy.

"Would somebody explain what is going on here?" Lucas Reed yelled.

Hannah felt the warmth of Jamie's hand on her shoulder and saw that his other hand clung to Cooper's shoulder. "It's quite simple, sir. Hannah almost married the wrong Reed brother. She loves Cooper, and she should marry him, not me."

Mrs. Reed stepped forward. "Cooper Reed, what is the meaning of this? How could you do such a horrible thing to your brother?" she cried.

Hannah held her breath, hoping that Heather Reed would

keep her Scottish temper under control.

Before Cooper could respond, Jamie jumped back into the discussion. "Don't you see, Mother? It makes good sense. You said yourself that Cooper hasn't been himself ever since we came back to Reed Springs. You said he was moping around like a lovesick puppy."

"Aye, I did. I thought he was pinin' away for some lassie back in England, but he had never mentioned a fondness for a young woman before."

Hannah's father turned a bewildered look toward Michael. "Just what do you know about all this?"

"I don't know how you and Mother couldn't see it. The two of them have been moping around ever since Jamie showed up. Haven't you seen the way they look at each other? I got curious the day Cooper and I rode to Charleston. I wondered why he was wearing my clothes. Then I put two and two together and realized that Hannah must have been taking care of him. No wonder she couldn't get over to Reed Springs fast enough each morning."

"It's true." Cooper smiled down at her and rubbed the scar on his forehead. "Hannah saved my life when she found me in the barn. I couldn't have lasted much longer."

Lucas Reed stepped forward. "This is all my fault. I strove too hard to make my boys close after what happened between Marcus and me. I see now that Cooper couldn't speak his mind for fear of hurting his brother." He turned to face his sons. "Forgive me if I went too far in establishing the family as most important."

Cooper smiled. "I forgive you, Father."

"Me, too." Jamie wrapped his arms around his father's and brother's shoulders.

Hannah's father turned to her. "Is it true? Are you in love with Cooper?"

"Oh yes, sir. So much that I thought I would die without

him." She shot Cooper a hesitant smile.

"Cooper Reed," Hannah's father bellowed, "just how did this happen? How could you steal my daughter's heart right out from under my nose?"

"It's a long story, sir, and I'm afraid it's my heart that *she* kidnapped," Cooper said, smiling completely for the first time in days.

❧

A short while later, Cooper and Hannah had replayed the whole story. Jamie still stood with his hands on their shoulders, offering silent support.

"So you see, sir, your daughter saved my life. I'd be dead right now if she hadn't come along and taken care of me."

Hannah smiled openly at the man she loved. He stood in front of her father just as bold as you please. The pride she felt that Cooper had the gumption to stand up to her father's inquisition was equaled only by her love for him.

"And do you love her as Jamie says?" Father asked, his hands fisted on his hips.

"Yes, sir, I love her with all my heart. I've been so distraught at the thought of losing her I was certain I would shrivel up and die. If you have no objections, Mr. Madison, I'd like to ask you for your daughter's hand in marriage." Cooper's gaze shot toward Jamie. "That is if my brother is willing to relinquish his claim to her."

Jamie pursed his lips and ducked his head, then looked around at those crowded around him. "This is probably my own fault. I should have put a halt to this sham engagement years ago."

His mother gasped and held her hand to her mouth, and Jamie sent her an affectionate smile. "I'm sorry to ruin your plans, Mum. I thought I could go along and would grow to love Hannah. I've always been fond of her, you know."

The melancholy smile he gave Hannah made her stomach

swirl. The last thing she wanted was to hurt him.

"But I don't love her—not as Cooper obviously does. They deserve a chance at happiness—a chance to be together. I only hope that one day I'll find a woman who cherishes me as much as Hannah does Coop."

Hope coursed through Hannah's veins, caressing her like warm milk on a cold night. Her dream might actually be realized. Her pleading eyes held her father's, and she saw him weighing all that he had just heard. He turned around and looked at the shocked expression on his wife's face. Then he turned and looked at the same bewilderment on Heather Reed's face. "Well, does anybody have any objections to Cooper and Hannah getting married?"

Nobody uttered a sound. The dark clouds suddenly parted, and long fingers of bright sunshine illuminated the area, sending golden rays of sunlight blasting straight into Hannah's heart.

"All right then, I guess we have a wedding to finish—or rather—start!"

"Take good care of her, little brother." Jamie gently squeezed Hannah's shoulder.

Hannah fell into Cooper's arms with a squeal. "*Trust Me,*" the Lord had said. As Coop enveloped her in his strong arms, she marveled at the way God had worked everything out. She had been willing to give up her dream, but God had resurrected it in a way she never thought possible.

❧

Cooper held Hannah tightly in his embrace, ignoring the gawking crowd of grinning spectators. "So, Hannah Caroline Madison," he whispered in her ear, "would you like to be *my* wife?"

"Oh yes, my love," she whispered. Tears—happy tears, he suspected—ran down her soft cheeks. "I can hardly wait."

Cooper leaned down and placed his lips on Hannah's as

all the pain and despondency he'd felt the past few days and weeks melted away.

"Hey," Michael yelled, "the preacher hasn't reached the kissing part yet!"

Cooper pulled back, temporarily interrupting their kiss. Hannah's wide, enthusiastic grin echoed his. The laughter around them softened as they pulled apart and turned toward the front.

The minister scratched his chin, and he shook his head as if he were trying to recover from the shocking chain of events. He took a long look at the crowd and then opened his Bible. "I'll begin reading from the second chapter of Genesis. 'But for Adam there was not found an help meet for him. And the Lord God caused a deep sleep to fall upon Adam, and he slept: and he took one of his ribs, and closed up the flesh instead thereof; And the rib, which the Lord God had taken from man, made he a woman, and brought her unto the man.'"

Cooper looked down at Hannah's astonished expression and knew it mirrored his. God had taken Adam—Cooper in this instance—amnesia, cracked ribs, and all, and used them to bring to him the woman who would become his wife today. He smiled at his angel and turned back to the minister, anxious to begin his married life.

A Letter To Our Readers

Dear Reader:

In order that we might better contribute to your reading enjoyment, we would appreciate your taking a few minutes to respond to the following questions. We welcome your comments and read each form and letter we receive. When completed, please return to the following:

Fiction Editor
Heartsong Presents
PO Box 719
Uhrichsville, Ohio 44683

1. Did you enjoy reading *Secrets of the Heart* by Vickie McDonough?
   ❏ Very much! I would like to see more books by this author!
   ❏ Moderately. I would have enjoyed it more if

   _____

   _____

   _____

2. Are you a member of **Heartsong Presents**? ❏ Yes ❏ No
   If no, where did you purchase this book? _____

   _____

3. How would you rate, on a scale from 1 (poor) to 5 (superior), the cover design? _____

4. On a scale from 1 (poor) to 10 (superior), please rate the following elements.

   ____ Heroine   ____ Plot
   ____ Hero   ____ Inspirational theme
   ____ Setting   ____ Secondary characters

5. These characters were special because? _____

_____

_____

6. How has this book inspired your life? _____

_____

_____

7. What settings would you like to see covered in future
   Heartsong Presents books? _____

_____

_____

8. What are some inspirational themes you would like to see
   treated in future books? _____

_____

_____

9. Would you be interested in reading other **Heartsong
   Presents** titles? ❑ Yes ❑ No

10. Please check your age range:
   ❑ Under 18   ❑ 18-24
   ❑ 25-34   ❑ 35-45
   ❑ 46-55   ❑ Over 55

Name _____

Occupation _____

Address _____

City, State, Zip _____

E-mail _____

Finally a Bride

Reporter Jacqueline Davis is suspicious of the new preacher. But will a budding romance overshadow her determination to uncover her secrets? Jailbird Carly Payton is looking for a new start in life. Garret Corbett is looking to avoid marriage with a jailbird. Will love blossom with a second look?

Romance, paperback, 320 pages, 5.5" x 8.375"